The Sacred Fury

By Barton and Elizabeth Cockey

DORRANCE
PUBLISHING CO
EST. 1920
PITTSBURGH, PENNSYLVANIA 15238

The contents of this work, including, but not limited to, the accuracy of events, people, and places depicted; opinions expressed; permission to use previously published materials included; and any advice given or actions advocated are solely the responsibility of the author, who assumes all liability for said work and indemnifies the publisher against any claims stemming from publication of the work.

This is a work of fiction. Names, characters, businesses, places, events and incidents are either the products of the author's imagination or used in a fictitious manner. Any resemblance to actual persons, living or dead, or actual events is purely coincidental.

Dorrance Publishing Co
585 Alpha Drive
Pittsburgh, PA 15238
Visit our website at *www.dorrancebookstore.com*

ISBN: 978-1-4809-9144-6
eISBN: 978-1-4809-9402-7

ALSO by Barton & Elizabeth Cockey

Upstate New York: Towns That We Love
Drawn to the Land: The Romance of Farming
Baltimore County: Historical Reflections &
Favorite Scenes
The Reincarnation of Piggy Pie Pooh
Untold Stories of the Battenkill

"I care not whether my work be read now or by posterity. I can afford to wait a century for readers when God himself has waited six thousand years for an observer. I triumph. I have stolen the golden secret of the Egyptians. I will indulge my sacred fury."

—Edgar Allan Poe, Eureka,
(quoting Johannes Kepler)

The Sacred Fury

Chapter 1

A bitter wind forced its way down Howard Street as the Light Rail train shivered to a halt just below Baltimore Street. Joe pulled his long coat closer around him as he stepped out onto the slushy pavement. The cold blast pushed him sideways. An airborne plastic grocery bag slapped against his face, then resumed its southward flight toward the icy Patapsco. The unnatural glow of the street lights seemed to subtract warmth instead of adding it. The wind tugged at his woolen cap, but his hand went up just in time to settle it more securely. As it did so, he became aware that he had forgotten to mend the hole in his right mitten.

He had been warm enough on the train ride from Hunt Valley. Wanda had left him near the northern terminus of the line, in the parking lot of the adjacent shopping mall, and given him specific instructions. He could not drive into Baltimore because "They have access to the security cameras, and the cameras are everywhere." He must not attract the attention of police or passersby. "No matter what, don't speak to anyone," she had instructed. And then she had winked and given him a push out the door. "Great care," she said; "take great care. If you have a problem or can't get a train to come back, go to the doctor's office."

He paused for a moment to be sure he had got off at the right stop and watched the vapor of his breath snatched away by the gale. There were others getting off the train too, and he waited for them to move along before he started walking up Howard Street towards Fayette. All the other passengers had headed south, toward the brighter lights of Camden Yards and the Convention Center, where some sports event or science fiction fantasy convention was under way. To the north, the street was empty, and the faces of the buildings were forbidding. Even the rats were inside tonight, he thought. He squinted against the blowing trash and road salt. Some of the taller buildings had lights in the upper stories. There were people in those places, living lives quite apart from his own. They were sitting down to dinner, watching the tube, indifferent to the gale and the cold weather. Safe.

As he turned left onto Fayette Street, the wind abated. He shook his head, clearing his mind. Stay on purpose, he said to himself. Stay. His mission was to find the grave, deliver the cognac and roses, and then wait. He was not exactly clear what it was that he was waiting for. That piece of information had not been given to him. All he knew was that he was to make the delivery and wait. He was to be the "toaster" that year, January 18 being the eve of the anniversary of Edgar Alan Poe's birth. It was an honor really, that such a simple man as he should have been chosen. And this was an agreement he had promised to keep no matter what.

"I am important," he repeated to himself as he trudged along. But as to why that was so, he had no idea. Repeating the phrase bolstered his spirits though, and he kept it up as he leaned into the wind. All he knew was that he was supposed to meet someone.

As he neared Greene Street, the howling of the wind increased, and he pulled his cap down so the its fuzzy edge shaded his eyes. A shadow seemed to move within deeper shadow on his left. Turning suddenly, he found he was looking up at a dark Gothic church tower. Nothing moved on the steps or behind the wrought-iron paling. Just past the tower was a small graveyard with an iron gate. The gate was wide open. Joe looked around to make sure no one was following him, then stepped inside the graveyard. He had never seen a cemetery like this before, almost entirely paved with brick and crammed with crypts and monuments. Where was the one he was supposed to find?

Turning a corner, he slipped on a patch of ice but caught himself just in time by reaching out for one of the monuments. The bright street lights cast dark shadows in this confined space, which seemed more and more like a jail, with its iron bars and brick walls. He looked back at the gate. It was shut! His heart began pounding. Who had closed it? He listened for footsteps. He thought he could hear a distant commotion somewhere outside the wall, then only the rush of the wind and a distant siren. And there it was again, angry voices yelling back and forth and bottles breaking. Someone screamed, and then he could hear people running. He stepped back into a shadow, suddenly glad to have a hiding place of sorts. He remained still, waiting for something to happen, but nothing did. The voices became fainter. A car's horn blared nearby, and he jumped.

Huddled in a corner now, he looked up at the building across the street, an elegant three-story brick structure with a comfortable, old-time feel to it. The other buildings in sight had a more austere look, with glaring glass and grim granite. Wanda had said that most of them belonged to the University of Maryland. As he looked, he thought he could see the newer buildings swallowing up the older ones. It was hard to believe that this spot was once at the very western end of the city, back when John Eager Howard was still alive. Joe knew that Howard was a hero of the American Revolution. The city had grown up around the little graveyard, and then, over a hundred years ago, Westminster Hall sprouted on top of the graveyard itself, and a sunless catacomb had devoured vaults that once basked in sun and bathed in rain. A few blocks west were the "projects". Though the hideous high-rise public tenements had come down, most of the blocks beyond Martin Luther King, Junior Boulevard were unsafe at any hour.

There was no mistaking which tomb was Poe's. It was the whitest and most prominent in the lot, with a round bronze bas-relief of the man himself and the name of its most illustrious occupant carved across the base. The names of Poe's wife Virginia and his mother-in-law Maria Clemm were on the stone too.

Joe decided to sit down on the sill of a grave. It was cold, but at least it gave him a chance to consider the task before him. From the pocket of his coat he pulled the bottle of cognac that he had been given to leave on Poe's grave, then decided to take a sip. What could it hurt, he asked himself? After all, it was bitterly cold, and the wind had picked up; he was freezing despite his wool coverings, and hungry besides. His mittens kept slipping off the stopper, but after a short struggle, he managed to dislodge the cork with his teeth. Just a little one, he told himself. Nobody had said the bottle had to be full when he left it.

The stuff in the bottle was much stronger than he expected, and it burned going down. Joe choked and began coughing. The sound of his own cough frightened him. He was supposed to keep quiet. What was that creaking noise in the far corner? He strained his eyes at the shadows. Nothing moved. The cognac gave him a warm feeling inside, and he began to feel equal to whatever surprise might await him. Another swig was what he needed, and there would still be a good bit left.

His seat on the stone was close to the ground, and a draft was finding its way down his neck. He turned up his collar and pulled down his hat again. From where he sat, he had a clear view of the Poe monument but of nothing else.

Joe never saw who grabbed him from behind, wrenching him to the frozen ground. He gaped in astonishment as the brick pavement came up to meet his numbed face. All he knew was that it was unbelievably cold on the bricks and that his nose had begun to bleed. Then a deeper darkness descended on him, and he remembered as a far-away voice Wanda's admonition: "No matter what, don't speak to anyone."

Chapter 2

Sidney looked out her office window at the morning sunshine. The grass was turning green, and bright yellow daffodils were blooming near the parking lot. The laughter of students filtered up from below. If she could open the window, she would be able to hear birds singing and breathe in some of the sweet air. But the huge glass pane had only a tiny section at the bottom that was once designed to open, and even that had been fastened shut. She had complained, and the complaint had been "escalated" past the maintenance officer ("They're all like that.") to his supervisor ("I will forward your concern to the committee.") to *his* supervisor ("All windows are to be kept closed for security and energy conservation. We take pride in our status as a safe and environmentally conscious campus. Tampering with the building shell or climate controls will result in disciplinary action.")

She turned back from the window and looked down at her desk, where a large pile of mail had been stacked by her administrative intern. She sighed and began opening the first letter with her fingernail, ripping along the top of the envelope, leaving jagged edges. It was another request from a not-for-profit organization called H.O.P.E. (Helping Others Pleases Everyone) asking if she would favor them with a keynote address at their annual meeting. It was the usual blather about how much they admired her work at the college where she had helped to orchestrate a comprehensive "Learn to read" program for underserved students.

What they did not know was that the program had failed, quite miserably in fact. The Community College of Baltimore County (CCBC) had raised enough grant money to bus school-aged children out from downtown to the campus in Essex, where they would receive remedial help. The program was voluntary. Despite an intensive outreach campaign, only two students had signed up, and the project was finally scrapped. The publicity had been good for the college, though. Local news outlets liked the emphasis on "the underserved." She had given interviews on the Public Broadcasting Service. Her deep caring for the less fortunate had been palpable. Now it seemed everyone nationwide was writing or emailing or tweeting, either to invite her in as a consultant on their next grant request or to inquire about her lecture fee schedule.

The key word had been "underserved." It packed so much meaning. Perhaps the next iteration should be "ill served" or "disserved," to emphasize the helplessness and victimhood of the oppressed. Ah, well, best to stick with the familiar. The truth was that she had questioned the effectiveness of a purely voluntary program from the outset, but the college had bene-fited by all the news it had generated and was already asking for more funding. Now she was in the unfortunate position of being necessary to the college's fundraising and marketing ef-forts, a task she had neither asked for nor wanted. She did not enjoy the limelight or the company of others. All she really wanted was to pursue her career as professor of literature and, if she ever got around to it, to write the Great American Fem-inist Novel, with a sensitive exploration of intersectionality[1].

She was married, but not happily so. Dylan had seemed so in tune with her when they first met. And so passionate! As Sidney thought back, she could even muster some distant memories of a time when they had shared something very special together. How long had it lasted? She could not re-member. Now life had devolved to the daily drudgery of fighting traffic to arrive on time at her glass cage, attending endless meetings where nothing of value was ever decided, then fighting traffic again, only to find a dull stranger across the dinner table, pecking at his I-phone over a microwaved meal. Dylan for his part didn't even notice their estrangement, or worse, she thought, didn't even care. Most of his communications with her were texted photos of whatever lavish lunch he had ordered in some trendy downtown eatery.

"Stop it, stop," she told herself. "If you always dwell on negative things, you'll go crazy!" She cradled her head with both hands and clenched her eyes shut. No tears, she thought; no self-pity. At least she had a husband that came home, helped provide a roof over their heads. They were saving up for a house and were hoping to live outside Baltimore City soon. It was only a matter of time.

Just a little while longer…

She leaned across the pile of mail and turned on her computer. The screen lit up instantly, and she watched as all the little icons came to life before her. She went directly to her college email account. There were usually several memos that required her attention, most of them related to gender and diversity issues, rules of conduct to avoid micro-aggressions, compliance training and the like. A few actually had to do with such ancillary matters as academics.

The first email was marked "Immediate Attention." The dean had drafted a letter to all department heads. Sidney clicked on the attachment and leaned closer to the screen.

Dear Colleagues,

I am writing to remind you of the Community College of Baltimore County's commitment to excellence, and desire to become a diversity compliant community, which is a goal I believe we all share. Today I am asking everyone for your continued support and encouragement, especially in our roles as educators, and community leaders. Our combined efforts are needed and wanted by all those who attend classes on campus or in off-site locations throughout Maryland.

Our faculty and student body reflect the diversity of gender identity, ethnicity, and national origin of our country as a whole. But our values and ideas are shared by all. We strive together toward a common goal: that being the welfare of all and the recognition of the equality of all. And with that end in view, I ask for more diligence in our common purpose, in all our communication between ourselves while at the same time acknowledging the needs of others not so privileged as ourselves.

Interpersonal interaction on or off campus must be always respectful of differences and awareness of white privilege. All dialogue must be honest in addressing the reality of racial inequality and institutional racism. Insensitivity in this area will not be permitted or tolerated. If anyone is privy to counter activity not so directed then I request and the dean of student affairs demands that all such indignance is reported directly to this office.

Failure to report such activity may be the severance of one's term and benefits, as if having committed the original misconduct. All actions or omissions that constitute an offense will be considered a 'hate crime' and against our mission here at the Community College of Baltimore County.

Our board of directors have directed this office to announce new policy changes effective immediately. That acting in such capacity and representing our esteemed staff of professors, teachers and advisors the college is putting into effect immediately a race compliant strategy that combines race sensitivity with special emphasis for any under achieving student of color.

Hence forth all male students of color shall be moved forward with passing grades irregardless of attendance and/or the ability to comprehend information presented in the classroom. In this manner, all students shall be raised to the same level of achievement and therefore receive the same opportunities for advancement in their chosen fields. If anyone has procedural questions or concerns please do not hesitate to contact me at the earliest convenience.

Truly yours.

Dean of Student Affairs, Dr. Remus Prada

Sidney read the letter again, not quite certain whether she had understood it correctly. Did the dean really mean that certain students would be guaranteed a passing grade regardless of merit? And, if this were in fact true, what would the final grade be? How would it be determined? She knew that the topic of a simple pass-fail system had been discussed and debated several months prior by the department heads and the dean of student affairs. The administration, or someone consulting with the administration, was questioning whether the current grading system was completely fair for those students whose work was not on a par with others receiving higher marks. It was Sidney's understanding that this unfairness could end up being a trigger for students who were less likely to comprehend the material being presented.

According to the dean, every student, regardless of achievement or aptitude, was to be considered equal in all aspects while attending the Community College of Baltimore County. This edict was confirmed by the State of Maryland's higher education office: all universities and colleges receiving funding for academic programs needed to be compliant or lose their funding. There was also a lurking fear that Federal criteria for civil rights violations were being revised to include disparate impact in grading. She looked out the window again. Everything still looked the same as it had before she read the letter. But she had the uncanny feeling that things were not the same at all, and perhaps CCBC would not ever again be what it was: an institution of higher learning.

This thought did nothing to improve her already dismal state of mind and led her back to thinking about her marriage to Dylan. She felt trapped in both her work and her marriage. After Dylan found a job at the *Baltimore Herald*, they had moved away from the cheerful little college town of Bryn Mawr in Pennsylvania. Dylan had graduated from Haverford with a degree in journalism but had been delivering pizza to college students after not finding suitable employment in the town. After numerous job applications, he had finally been able to land a part time position writing for the weekend Home & Garden section of the *Philadelphia Eagle*. At that time, Sidney was just finishing her master's degree in English literature at Bryn Mawr College. They had met through an internet dating service and gotten married in rather a hurry. He had known all about Derrida and Foucault[2] and was not at all chauvinistic or assertive about his masculinity. After several weeks of hot lovemaking and passionate, late-night discussions of the implications of post-structuralism for gender relations in the 21st century, marriage had seemed the obvious next step. Wrong. Wrong. She returned to holding her head in her hands.

At length, pulling herself up by sheer force of will, she stood with her face to the window. Deep breaths. Clear your thoughts. Let nature heal your… *Thunk!* A robin flew headlong against the glass, leaving a wet smudge and a few downy feathers where it had struck. Sidney jumped back, upsetting the small digital clock on her desk. When she picked it up, she saw that she had barely enough time to run across campus to her first class, English 101. She turned off the computer and picked up her things, along with the assigned text: *The Bedford Guide for College Writers*.

As she made her way out of the building and along the concrete walk, she began to wonder whether some of her minority students would be triggered by the book. She had been depressed, but this new thought made her nervous. Weren't grammar, rhetoric and logic just part of the system of oppression put in place by the white male power structure, a subtle tool designed to humiliate people of color? She was pretty sure that she had heard a recent guest speaker at the college say something to that effect. He had spoken with great authority, having received a Genius Grant from some foundation or other. How did that black genius's analysis, which she supposed must be true, mesh with the announcement so recently put forth by the dean?

Proposition 1: My course material is inherently racially insensitive because it is part of the system of oppression.
Proposition 2: Racial insensitivity is a firing offense.

Maybe the two ideas didn't mesh. But what if they did? She pictured the ideas as gigantic gears moving into alignment and began to imagine that she was looking through a trapdoor into the works of some massive machine and shuddered at the thought of getting caught between the teeth of those relentless, impersonal gears. *Haaaawnk!* She stepped back just in time to avoid being hit by a yellow Volkswagen.

Far across town and a short distance from the Inner Harbor stood the building which housed the *Baltimore Herald*. The paper had sold its brick and glass headquarters after being taken over by another news outlet. Most of the staff had been let go years before, and the now antiquated presses had been carted off like so much scrap metal. Now the whole operation was consolidated into the sixth and seventh floors of a mirrored glass high-rise with a view of the harbor. Dylan had been lucky to apply for a position just as the elderly and much-beloved Gaston McManus was being carried out on a gurney.

Gaston, who affected a continental air and always wore a beret, had an encyclopedic knowledge of Old Baltimore— the architecture, the art scene, the theatre, and the families whose doings had graced the Society pages in those long-ago days when it was acceptable for a paper to have Society pages. His southern roots and his sentimental attachment to the city's historic monuments would probably have lost him his job ages ago if he had not been openly gay, with a large following in the city's artsy demimonde. A more politically correct replacement had been contemplated for some time, preferably someone with no connection to the deplorable Old Baltimoreans whose ancestors the Union army had had to hold at gunpoint throughout the Civil War. And of course, an entry-level salary would be far more acceptable to management. The callow and rather desperate young applicant fresh from Haverford would do nicely.

Dylan had been told that his new job was contingent on his ability to write interesting articles about real estate in Baltimore. He had been assigned to this department based upon his experience at the *Philadelphia Eagle*. Dylan had been given the title of Junior Editor. He bridled a little at the "junior" part, but at least it meant that he had his foot well inside the door. He was to inherit Gaston's small, cramped cubby, which was enclosed on three sides by temporary partitions upholstered in gray material very similar to the industrial-style carpeting that covered the floors.

The first six months of his employment were probationary and supposedly under the supervision of the fellow in the next cubicle, Senior Editor Jack Grimmes, life style editor for the *Herald*. He was an older man who dressed flamboyantly, with an open-neck shirt and a silk scarf tied loosely about his neck. Dylan had had the pleasure of meeting Jack on his first day, but that had been several months ago. Since then he had seen little of the man, although his columns continued to appear on a regular basis in the *Herald*. Dylan found to his surprise that he was often expected to edit Grimmes' copy, which he did, albeit grudgingly. It wasn't fair, but

Dylan's college education had provided him with a template to fit all such impositions into a more general pattern of exploitation of the young by the old, the weak by the strong, and the minority by the majority. The older concept of apprenticeship was not part of his understanding of the world.

Dylan therefore accepted this unfairness with a bitter cynicism that gave him two satisfying marks on his inner ledger: one for his own status as a martyr to injustice and another for a debt incurred by his employer. He did not quite tell himself, "They owe me one," but he savored the taste of the debt. It freed him from any sense of obligation or loyalty. The walls of his cubby still had clippings and photographs left behind by old Gaston: group photographs of the reporter in chummy poses with smiling grandees in evening dress, their faces flushed with drink; clippings of reviews extolling the unique queerness of some nightclub; pictures of a brick church surrounded by big buildings. Management had told Dylan not to touch anything because Gaston would be back to claim his belongings; but months had passed, and here he was trying to work at what was still quite clearly someone else's desk. The cheap black vinyl swivel chair had lost an arm, and the height adjustment gradually lost altitude as the day wore on. Swiveling made it sink faster, so he tried to keep still as he searched the internet for background information on his new home town. Every few minutes, Dylan checked his email lest he miss an important meeting or fresh copy from Jack. Most days, he left the cubicle only for lunch.

Early on, Dylan had hoped to meet some of the other employees by eating his lunch in the common room, but so far, he had found the other newspaper staff rather stand-offish. He was not sure whether they viewed him as a threat or as a mere temporary employee, not worth the investment of their precious time until his position was settled. Snatches of conversation that he overheard suggested a general sense of insecurity about the future of the industry. "It's all going to be on-line in a few years." "Paperless. Everything is headed for paperless."

Every day Dylan would take his lunch, a chicken salad sandwich and chips, down to the common room. He would then select a little packet of French roast, insert it in the coffee machine, and watch the brown liquid dribble into his paper cup. Finding a place to sit was the awkward part. It seemed that nearly everyone was already part of some group, and those groups all sat together. So, Dylan sat by himself at a table in the back, next to the windows looking out on the city of Baltimore below. The good thing was that he had a tremendous view of the downtown, Inner Harbor and Federal Hill. The first week, he had done his best to appear not to care that no one else seemed interested in joining him. Then, just when he had resigned himself to solitary lunches, a chubby young man with a shock of unruly red hair approached him.

He was carrying a couple of steaming boxes that exuded aromas of cumin and garlic.

"Hey, I'm Glen. Want some Indian? I scored some really good shit today." He opened a cellophane packet and dumped a paper napkin and some white plastic utensils on the table. Sitting down across from Dylan, he popped open one of the boxes, plunged the plastic fork into what looked like a mix of brown rice, chick peas, shrimp, and onions, and began shoveling the food into his mouth. "Mmm! Grab the spoon and try some. New place just opened up. Not too far from here."

Dylan hesitated, not because the fare was unappealing, but because as Glen spoke, he sprayed bits of rice back into the open container.

"Thanks," said Dylan, "That looks really good. Can I try some of what's in the other box?"

"Go for it," urged Glen cheerfully. At the word "go," a chickpea, as if impelled from the starting gate, popped out of Glen's mouth and onto the table. Too sticky to roll, it lay where it landed. Dylan moved the other box a little closer to himself and, as he hoped, out of range.

Glen ignored the escaped pea and went on chattering amiably. It seemed that Glen's job was in the advertising department, which was located one floor down. But he wasn't as lucky as Dylan, he said. He didn't have his own cubicle but sat in a large room at a desk with a phone and an old laptop computer, with a few others who also sat at desks with phones and laptops. All he did all day was make telephone calls to businesses about taking out advertisements in the Herald. Once he secured a commitment, he would send the client instructions from his computer with a link to the art department, where the ad copy and layout would be completed and returned to the business via the internet. It was a boring job too, he told Dylan. "How'd ya like to talk on the phone all day, but never see anybody?" he asked. "You are lucky to be a cube," he finished.

Dylan hadn't realized that employees on his own floor were commonly referred to as "cubes".

Within a week, Glen had begun eating lunch with Dylan on a fairly regular basis. Glen had been at the Herald for a couple of years and took pride in explaining how the various departments functioned, at least in relationship to one another, and more importantly, how it was possible to stretch the thirty minutes allotted for lunch to sneak out of the building and eat for free at some of the restaurants nearby. Glen seemed to have found a way around everything. He had worked out how to bypass the building's security by taking the freight elevator, not because there was any real need to do so but because he could.

"Hey, guy, lemme show ya how to get out of this joint and get some real food for a change," Glen had said after the doors of the elevator had shut behind them. They rode all the way down to the basement. It was dark, and there was a rancid smell coming from somewhere that Dylan couldn't identify. A shallow stream of water coursed along the floor. There was only one exit door, painted yellow, with a sign saying "Emergency exit only. Alarm."

Dylan hadn't liked the looks of it at all and wanted to get back to his desk without drawing any attention to himself, but Glen had talked him out of it. "C'mon, man. Here's how you keep the alarm from going off and jam the lock so we can get back in. I wanna take you to a place called Gitmos where they make great sub sandwiches." Dylan shrugged and looked down at the concrete floor. Around his shoes, little puddles of oil shimmered with red and blue and green under the fluorescent lighting. "I don't know. I don't want to get into any trouble or be late getting back," he said.

"It beats eating the same thing every day," Glen replied. And so, Dylan had followed him out the exit and into the daylight. Squinting his eyes to adjust to the brightness, he began to see a dark, old brick building across the street with a blue-and-white sign for "Gitmos Deli."

"I just realized I don't have any cash on me," Dylan said, "and I really can't afford to eat out every day."

Glen smiled. "We don't need any money, buddy. You eat for free when you eat with me!"

After that, it was easy, and Dylan had begun taking food photos on his I-phone. Glen had a smooth way about him and quickly ingratiated himself with the proprietors of all the local eating establishments. He had as many lines as there were restaurants. "Our paper would love to run a story on your place here." "I'm authorized to cut you a deal on advertising." "The Herald is holding a catered soiree, and I've been assigned the tough job of sampling the food. Heh, heh." Dylan wasn't sure whether any of Glen's claims were true, but no one seemed to want to risk offending the Baltimore Herald. The name of the paper still carried a certain authority, even if its fiscal prospects were shaky.

The idea that there was something sneaky about Glen's lunchtime adventures quickly gave way to an admiration for the salesman's charm and savoir faire. "Get them laughing," Glen liked to say, "and they'll want to do you a favor." Dylan began to feel more clever himself, just by association, and he began to hope that eventually he would fit into an inner circle of some kind, and tell anecdotes and impress everyone with his intelligence and wit. He had even begun to be more confident emailing back and forth to Jack about a story they had been assigned to write together. Then, this very day, Jack dropped by the cubicle unannounced, to leave photos to be included in his next column.

Jack stood particularly close to Dylan, as if to impart confidential information. Dylan could smell his cologne and see the curly hairs that protruded from the top of his shirt, weaving their way through a thick gold chain. "That last article you wrote, the one about 33rd Street, was brilliant. I had a realtor call me, one of the top earners, to say that she was getting dozens of calls from yuppies wanting to buy there. I do believe you've driven the prices up overnight! Breath mint?" The senior editor paused to pop a mint into his mouth and looked Dylan up and down in an appraising sort of way. "Mm. Yes," he said, drawing even nearer. "I like what I see. At last a young protégé worthy of my tutelage." With a wink, he spun round and swept out of the cubicle.

"Yes! I'm in!" thought Dylan.

$\mathcal{C}$hapter 3

Sidney was shaking when she went out to her car at the end of the day. She glanced behind her as she unlocked the door, threw her books and purse onto the passenger seat, jumped in and pressed the lock button. *Clunk.* Safe for the moment. She tried to remember exactly what had happened in her classroom. English 101 was a remedial course designed to teach basic reading and writing skills to those who had not learned them in high school. The pupils came from a variety of backgrounds. Her last assignment for the class had been to write an essay on a topic in the day's news. One student, Tameesha, had selected an article in the Washington Post about under-representation of blacks in Hollywood movies and Oscar nominations. Her essay was a combination of cut-and-paste of the Post article and angry assertions about slavery and segregation. Today, Sidney had handed the corrected papers back to the students. She had made some general remarks about common errors, stressing the difference between honest citation of a source and plagiarism. She had also emphasized that a critical reader learns to discriminate between facts and opinions. At the end of the class, Tameesha and her friend Lamar had come up to Sidney with scowls on their faces.

"You give me a D!" shouted Tameesha, waving her paper. "And you write on my paper I di'nt have no right to bring up slavery!"

"That's not what I wrote," said Sidney. "I wrote that you had not established a connection between the current topic and the topic of slavery."

"I said it be just like slavery!"

"Well, Tameesha, if it is just like slavery, you haven't explained why. Think about it. I mean, these are very well-paid movie stars. Nobody owns them. Nobody owns you. We don't have slavery in America anymore. If you want to make a case that the Oscars are like slavery, you need to explain yourself better than you did. You need to explain why…"

"I gots to 'splain. *I* gots to 'splain! You white people, you make up all the rules, and you jus' tell us black people what to do!" She shook the paper in Sidney's face.

This hostile outburst had a surprising effect on Sidney.

Welling up from deep in her heart came a profound sympathy for this girl and a conviction that here was an opportunity to reach out and help a mind in need, a mind that would go to waste without some kindly guidance. "Look," said Sidney, "I know you want to get your ideas across, but if you want to persuade others, you must put your argument together so that the facts or assertions are *connected*. Like links in a chain. If the links don't connect, the argument falls apart. Try rewriting the essay so that the reader can follow your chain of ideas." She smiled a warm smile, pleased with herself for finding a simple analogy that avoided the difficult subject of logic.

"You can't talk to me that way. That's racist," snarled Tameesha.

Lamar smiled unpleasantly and leaned toward Sidney. He pointed his finger in her face and said,

"She gon' report yo' ass! Oh, yeah. She gon' git you!"

Sidney arrived home after two hours in traffic. There had been an accident on Northern Parkway; and as she edged her car along, she saw a fire truck, several ambulances and many police cars. Everyone in front of her was slowing down to look. It made her angry. She didn't understand the callousness of people, gawking at the suffering of others.

When at last she arrived back at the apartment on Roland

Avenue, it was nearly dark. She parked her car in the lane behind the house, locked the car, and unlocked the back gate. Her landlady, Mrs. Fitzgerald, was standing in the backyard with a gardening trowel in her hand while her three Pekingese dogs snuffled about, urinating and defecating in the flower beds. Sidney pursed her lips. She despised dogs, especially little yappy, poopy things.

As she passed through the gate, her handbag hung up on the chain-link fence. There were too many locks, she thought, part of the whole system of separation of peoples that afflicted the world at large, preventing true understanding. The tyranny of walls and borders. But the landlady insisted on locking the back gate, citing recent break-ins down the block and warnings from the police.

When Sidney closed the back gate behind her, the dogs stopped what they were doing and came charging at her, jumping up gleefully, whining and wagging their tails. Their sharp little claws scratched her legs. "Ow! Stop that!" she barked. Mrs. Fitzgerald clapped her hands and called, "Come, my preciouses!" When the little beasts ignored the command, she added, "I have treats". The words had an instant effect, and all three of the brutes ran back to Mrs. Fitzgerald, who was rummaging in her apron pocket.

Sidney approached the group of dogs and their mistress with caution. "Welcome home, my dear," Mrs. Fitzgerald said brightly. "Did you have a long day at work again?"

Sidney sighed and put her parcels down before answering. "There was a confrontation about an assignment in class." It seemed inappropriate to be any more specific. Average people were apt to draw the wrong conclusion if they heard about scholastic issues involving minorities. There was enough prejudice about already. No sense in feeding it. "And then there was a bad accident on the way home," she said. "But thank you for asking, Mrs. Fitzgerald."

Mrs. Fitzgerald smiled maternally. "Please just call me Rose," she said. "We all live here together now, and we're rather like house-mates aren't we?"

She had a point, because the house was a two-family affair, one apartment above the other, with a shared basement where the laundry was done. Sidney and Dylan lived in the second-floor apartment, which had a balcony overlooking the back yard, while the owners, the Fitzgeralds, occupied the first floor, with a porch on the street side. The balcony was perhaps the main reason they had decided to rent the apartment in the first place. It gave them the privacy Sidney enjoyed, away from the noise of the city street. "Never buy a house on a street with a double yellow line," her aunt used to say. Well, here they were, but she wasn't buying, not here. The tenants could wash and dry clothes on Sundays, Wednesdays and Fridays. So far, this arrangement had not been too difficult, and they also shared the long, narrow, tree-shaded back yard. Still, Sidney felt strange calling her landlady by her first name. It seemed wrong because it might possibly give the impression of being too familial. She felt that it was important for her own autonomy that they keep their relationship more on a professional basis. She didn't want to become friends with this woman, still less with her husband. What if they started to ask them down for dinner? She didn't want to have to explain why Dylan had started to come home very late most nights, having important assignments or business meetings at the *Herald*.

Mrs. Fitzgerald stepped closer to Sidney, placing a hand on her shoulder. The dogs maintained a polite distance, having been driven back by a shushing from Mrs. Fitzgerald and a hand signal that was dog sign language for stay or sit, Sidney couldn't remember which. "You seem so tired," Mrs. Fitzgerald said. "Would you like to come down after you've settled your things and have a nice cup of Chai tea with me?"

This suggestion created a moment of panic in Sidney. "Not tonight, I'm afraid," Sidney said. "I've a monstrous load of assignments to correct. Perhaps some other time."

Mrs. Fitzgerald frowned a little before opening the basement door to let the dogs run in. "Well, perhaps some other time then, dear. I'm always available if you'd like to chat, right downstairs, you know!" She locked the deadbolt behind them, and both women threaded their way through the cluttered cellar and climbed the creaky stairs. The dogs had already run up to the first floor and were wagging and jumping as they waited to be let in. Sidney bade them all a happy evening before climbing the next flight of stairs and fishing out her keychain. Too many locks, too many keys. She found the key with the purple tag and let herself in.

Dylan had sent her a text earlier, while she was still in class: *Important meeting tonight, Home late. XO.* She had already decided to eat dinner without him and to try to turn in early. But first, she reached into her purse, digging around until she found a small bottle from the pharmacy. It was only a generic, over-the-counter sleeping pill, but she hoped it would work. She had been having nightmares of late, waking in a cold sweat long before sun-up. The nightmares, coupled with her responsibilities at school, had begun to take a toll. Then, yesterday, she had seen an old friend from high school walking down Roland Avenue at dusk. He had waved to her and then disappeared. Not stepped out of sight. Vanished. When she Googled his name, she had found his obituary, dated last week. Was she losing her mind? She didn't know anymore, and she missed her husband. At least she missed the man she had known before they had moved to Baltimore.

Not bothering to go into the kitchen to find something to eat, she uncorked a bottle of red wine, a nice Merlot. She popped the little pill into her mouth, and not bothering to pour the wine into a glass, drank directly from the bottle. Returning to the bedroom, she set the bottle down on the nightstand. Then she took off her clothes, throwing them into a pile on a chair by the dresser. Reflected in the mirror, her naked body was still lithe and beautiful. Why had her husband lost interest? A long t-shirt of Dylan's lay draped around a bedpost. She pulled it on. It smelled like him, and she felt its soft caress. Then she crawled under the covers and lay on her back, facing the ceiling. Somewhere, she had read that this position promoted deeper sleep. Worth a try.

A scratching at the bedroom window awoke her almost as soon as she had begun to doze. There was a shadowy, claw-like shape moving just outside, barely discernible; the window glass was frosted for privacy. Surely this spectral claw was only a branch of the tree next to the house. The brightest light in the room was the clock on the dresser. It was only 7:30pm, but it was dark outside; and she wondered whether it should be so dark this early. Throwing the covers back, she crept to the French doors at the back of the room and parted the curtains. Seeing nothing amiss, she decided to go out onto the balcony. Somebody might be creeping around out there. After all, Mrs. Fitzgerald had said that homes on the same block had been broken into several times in the last year. As she pulled the door open, a cold west wind blew a scattering of leaves into the room. She barely noticed the roar of the police heli-copter circling overhead; like the sirens, it had become part of the background pattern of everyday things. Dark clouds covered the sky. To the north, in the narrow, shadowy space between the houses, a pine tree and a big holly waved their arms in a weird dance. There were no lights next door.

Dylan returned sometime in the middle of the night. He tried to get into bed quietly, so as not to disturb his wife. It was the last thing he needed right now, to wake Sidney up. She had recently been complaining of having disturbing dreams and had been afraid to go to sleep. The dreams had been the main topic of discussion at the breakfast table over the last few weeks, so that Dylan could no longer take any pleasure in his morning coffee. Sidney had grown morose and irri-table, probably due to a lack of sleep, Dylan told himself. When he tried to reassure her that dreams are meaningless, she became angry and said that he was diminishing and dis-counting her. When he asked what she thought they meant, she said he had no business trying to analyze her. In fact, he was beginning to think he really didn't understand Sidney at all, or women in general for that matter. Maybe they had mar-ried too quickly before really getting to know each other, or maybe moving into the city of Baltimore had not been a very good idea in the first place.

But it was too late now to change those decisions. He rolled onto his side, turning away from her and moving closer to the edge of the bed. At least for now, he had to stay the course, especially since he finally felt that he was getting somewhere at the *Herald*. He was really making headway, both socially and professionally. After all, hadn't Jack just dropped by and given his writing high marks? Dylan knew that he was not bragging when he told himself that he was a persuasive, eloquent, even brilliant writer, finally ready to do something important. He was sure he could look forward to future assignments that would get him promoted to senior editor. Why did his wife have to spoil his success with her neuroses?

On the other hand, he had begun to doubt his ability to be a good husband, not just to Sidney, but to anybody. He was starting to feel hemmed in by domestic rules, like having to call if he could not be home at a certain hour. He resented her irritation when he got home late because of meetings, or because had joined his new-found friend to 'toss down a few beers,' as Glen liked to say. He also worried about the responsibility of paying the rent, the electric bill, the car insurance, the credit card balance, and all the other crazy expenses that appeared out of nowhere, wiping out whatever he had managed to save for the future. As he finally drifted off to sleep, he remembered all the pretty girls he had met on one of his and Glen's latest outings. "They love ya, buddy," Glen had said. "If I were you, I'd give one of them little honeys your business card."

Dylan woke up to birds chirping outside the bedroom window, and he could smell coffee brewing. Sidney must be up already! He dressed quickly, ran a comb through his hair, and hurried toward the kitchen. His hope was that this morning Sidney would be in a good mood. After all, it was Saturday, and neither of them had to go to work. He thought fondly about other weekends early in their marriage when they used to stay in bed until noon, and he would read the newspaper out loud to her.

He found her sitting at the dining room table, still in her bathrobe, holding a cup of coffee. There were dark circles under her eyes. She was clenching her mug in one hand and wiping tears from her face with a wadded-up paper towel in the other. "I can't take it anymore," she said.

"What's the matter?" he asked, not really wanting to know what the matter was.

"I've dreamed about that man again, the one that I see falling in a graveyard. First, he's falling, and then some people are dragging him into a vault deep in the earth. The vault is underneath an old church, and it's surrounded by lots of other graves. It's dark."

Dylan clenched his teeth. Sidney's dream was always the

same, and he was beginning to tire of hearing the same stupid story again. "I think you need to see someone, professionally I mean," he said.

Sidney began crying again. "But you don't understand," she said.

"*What* don't I understand?" asked Dylan. He stood with his arms crossed, waiting for a reply. Instead of answering, Sidney picked up the morning paper, which was opened to the local news section. There, on the inner pages of the *Herald* was a small black-and-white photo of Westminster Hall in downtown Baltimore with a caption that read: **Unsolved Missing Person Case Reopened By Family.** "So what," he said. "What's that got to do with anything?"

"It's the place that I keep dreaming about," she said.

*C*hapter 4

It was a sunny day, and a mild, moist breeze was wafting up the Jones Falls valley. The narrow valley was choked with old factory buildings, railroad tracks, and the six-lane Jones Falls Expressway. And the expressway was choked with traffic. Somewhere beneath the concrete pavement flowed the eponymous stream. Dylan rolled down his car window and inhaled the spring air. The wind carried with it a savor of salt that had drifted all the way from the Chesapeake and was somehow making itself known above the exhaust of hundreds of cars. The smell of the tidewater summoned images of ships weighing anchor and shaking out their sails, the green water swirling and foaming under their bowsprits. Ahead, far down the bay, was the open sea and freedom. Ah, freedom! He had never before been so relieved to return to work. Even though the traffic was barely moving, he was suddenly relaxed, almost elated. The weekend had begun badly, with a pointless upset about a dream that just coincidentally involved some old church downtown. He had not disguised his irritation, and his wife had become glum and silent. He was okay with "for better or for worse" as long as there was some *better*. Lately it seemed to be all worse.

The car ahead of him suddenly came to a complete stop. Dylan hit his brakes, just avoiding a collision. Well, he thought, things don't always go along easily. All you can do is keep on as best you can. The driver ahead of him appeared to have stalled her engine. He could hear the starter grinding. It was a small, Jeep-like vehicle, no doubt with a manual transmission. The bumper stickers were of a type that Dylan found congenial: *God Bless Everyone, No Exceptions*; *CO-EXIST* spelled out in a miscellany of mutually incompatible religious symbols; *My Body, My Choice*. "She and I could have a dialogue," he thought. The cars up ahead were moving forward. Someone behind him blared a horn. There were no openings for a lane change. A metaphor for his life. Some crazy female impeding him and nothing he could do about it. Not that he meant anything stereotypical or male-chauvinistic by such a thought. He mentally apologized to the driver ahead of him, then smiled unexpectedly; he was almost deliriously grateful to be able to get the hell out of the apartment for a while, and to have a job to go to.

"Here we all are," he said to himself as he drew in another lung-full of ozone. "We're all in this together!" The idea seemed inexplicably funny. Ms. Coexist had managed to get her car in gear, and they were moving again.

He leaned forward and turned on the radio. *The Morning Show* was on the local NPR station, and they were getting ready to go to a news and sports break. He turned up the volume to listen for the latest on the Orioles. It had been all over the media for the last several days. Today was to be Opening Day at Camden Yards, with the Governor of Maryland scheduled to throw out the first ball. The game wasn't supposed to start until 2 o'clock that afternoon, but NPR was reporting that city traffic would be heavy. There was also "grave concern" about demonstrations. Spokespersons for Black Lives Matter had been picketing the ball park for the last several days, denouncing baseball as a "white man's sport" that embodies "bourgeois values aimed at repressing people of color." Last Thursday night, someone had splashed red paint on the statue of Babe Ruth outside the stadium.

The radio announcer was interviewing the Police Commissioner, who said that there had been "credible threats" of violent disruption of the game. "We have reason to believe that the playing of the National Anthem may trigger a demonstration by activists, and we are determined to insure the safety of all those attending the game. Our fear is that violent

right-wing elements such as neo-Nazis and white supremacists may clash with peaceful protesters. For this reason, security measures have been tightened, and lines may be longer
at the gates. Fans are encouraged to arrive two hours earlier
than usual and should be prepared to have all their belongings
searched." The announcer was saying that the threat level was
so high that additional security forces would be provided by
a non-profit organization. Rumors were circulating that UN
peacekeeping troops were being flown in, but city officials
dismissed such stories as unfounded. "The only outside organization participating in safety measures will be the non-
partisan humanitarian group Global Outreach Organizing for
Diversity (GOOD)."

There was a taped official statement from last week; the
press secretary for the Mayor's Office was reading an announcement from Baltimore's Mayor Catherine Scatt. "A statue
of a white man with a baseball bat can be terrifying to a person
of color. Our people have suffered so many centuries of oppression that images of that nature can be literally terroristic. There
is no place for tolerance of terrorism and oppression."

A little while later, Dylan was comfortably ensconced in his
cube. He took a sip of coffee and turned on his computer to
see if he had received any urgent emails. If there had been a

window for him to stare out of, he would have done so; but instead he gazed at a framed photograph of Sidney on their honeymoon. He turned it face-down and closed his eyes to savor the coffee. The morning drive had mysteriously restored his verve and self-confidence. Today would be the beginning of newer and greater things. When he opened his eyes, he was instantly rewarded by an email from Jack. The subject line read, "IMPORTANT," and the message was, "Phone me at home as soon as you get this!"

Dylan sensed that the message called for confidentiality. He glanced across the narrow corridor at Doris, the administrative assistant. She glanced back. Dylan stood up as casually as he could manage and logged out of the computer. He decided it would be best to call Jack from his cell phone. He pushed in his chair and ambled down the corridor that led to the common room. Nobody was around. Slouching in a blue plastic chair near the door, he dialed Jack, who answered on the first ring.

"I'm sick," Jack moaned, rather breathlessly. There was a pause and then Jack continued speaking after what sounded like retching.

"Gee whiz, you must have a stomach flu," Dylan said.

"Yes, exactly," Jack said. Then he began another round of coughing and retching. Dylan waited, head down. He wondered whether this revolting performance might not be Jack's way of making an excuse for not writing his column, so that he could skip out to the Orioles' Opening Day. But Jack's urgent tone quickly persuaded him otherwise. "Sorry to put this on you, but I think this could be big. There's a meeting that I was going to cover, about the sale of Westminster Hall and Graveyard. It's owned by the University of Maryland, right down by the Thurgood Marshall Law Library. It's a major Baltimore landmark, mainly because it's where Edgar Allan Poe is buried. An outfit called GOOD, Global something something, is trying to buy it for redevelopment. I think this could be a hot story: clash of cultures, tradition versus modernization, etcetera." Dylan inadvertently scratched his head. Hadn't he just heard that name, GOOD, this morning on the radio?

"What I need you to do for me is attend that meeting this afternoon. It's at the law school. I'm pretty sure it's in a conference room in the library," Jack said. "I left my media pass with all the details and directions in a manila envelope on my desk. You can put your name on the pass instead of mine. Oh, and one more thing: you'd better leave early and walk. Opening Day is going to make it nearly impossible to park anywhere near the stadium." There was another bout of gagging and retching before the phone connection went dead. Dylan swore to himself. His cell phone's reception inside the building was often intermittent.

He was half-way through fixing himself another cup of coffee when he remembered that he hadn't finished the first one. His mind was running ahead of him. This assignment would be big. He could feel it. All the right elements were there: a connection to local history (not that he cared anything about that stuff, but some people still did); a connection to important officials from the city, the university, and this mysterious GOOD; and money! Somebody had a lot of moolah if they were looking to purchase this piece of property! This was auspicious, he thought, a chance to get a story, if there was one, and write something completely of his own! He'd be senior editor in no time. Or maybe something even better would open up!

His heart was pounding as he carried his coffee back to his desk. A quick glance confirmed that Jack's envelope was right where it was supposed to be. He logged back onto the computer and tried to concentrate on the puff piece that he needed to write about a fabulously expensive high-rise condo on the other side of the Harbor.

———————————————

Sidney stood in the kitchen with a cup of coffee. She took a tentative sip from the mug and winced; it was much too hot. She put it back down on the countertop and poured some more cream, watching as it swirled and sank. She paused, spoon in hand. "What if I don't stir it?" she thought. "What if I just let it cool off?" She realized that she was not thinking about the coffee at all. It was simple; she just needed a day off to compose herself after the recent upset in her classroom. The kids would have time to reconsider their attitude. She looked down at her cell phone. Not once in her short career had she called in sick. Bad karma. Say you're sick, and you'll get sick. "This is different," she told herself. "I really do need a mental health day." She held her breath and dialed the college's main number.

A recording of a woman's voice answered the phone. "Your call is being transferred. Please wait on the line." There was a ring tone, followed by "Thank you for calling the Community College of Baltimore County. Please hold for just a few moments until a representative is available to take your call. For your convenience, CCBC information is available 24-7 on our website, at www.ccbcmd.edu." Elevator music followed, then a voice that said, "Please continue to hold for the next available representative." The music resumed. After a few more repetitions of this message, Sidney hung up and searched her purse for the piece of paper that she had saved with the number of her department head. It took several more attempts, with someone answering, "please hold," and then repeatedly losing her connection; but after a half hour, she succeeded in excusing herself from classes. Of course, she hadn't actually asked for a mental health day. Rather, she remembered that someone had told her that "diarrhea" was a sure winner in situations like this, and someone had been right. Although her conscience gnawed at her for lying, she felt fairly confident that she hadn't jinxed herself with diarrhea.

Her next call was to her intern, Karen, who answered the phone, "Professor Sidney Morgan-Greene's office!" It was pleasant to hear this cheerful young voice announcing her married last name. The hyphenation had been a good idea. It made her sound more important, and it maintained her independence. She was Ms. Morgan-Greene, but Dylan was just Mr. Greene. Switching the cell phone to speaker, she said in a strained tone, "I'll be brief because I am not feeling well this morning and won't be coming in today. Please cancel all my classes."

"Yes, Ma'am," the intern said. "I hope you feel better."

"Thank you so much," Sidney replied. A touch of her finger ended the call. Then she walked into the living room and collapsed into the nearest chair, out of breath from the excitement of playing hooky. Her guilt was giving way to relief. In a strange sort of way, she felt proud of herself too. "I'm in charge of my life," she said over and over, as if repeating that phrase would make it so.

She didn't know how long she had sat there, but her coffee was cold when she took another sip. She could hear banging downstairs. Someone was knocking at the front door of the house. She got up and pulled her robe together before opening the apartment door. When she got halfway down the stairs, she could see that Mrs. Fitzgerald had entered the hall before her and was already advancing toward the front entrance. After looking through the peep hole, the landlady opened the door. Outside on the step stood a tall policeman wearing a dark blue uniform; his badge and holstered gun were in clear view. His eyes were shaded by the visor of his cap. Sidney froze in place. In panic, she wondered whether the college had detected her lie and called the police. The cop seemed to be looking right at her.

Mrs. Fitzgerald however, answered the door brightly. "How may I help you, officer?" she asked.

"We are conducting a safety inspection of the neighborhood," he said, "and I need to come in to see if this household has smoke detectors and is fire-safety compliant." He leaned forward towards the door as if to come inside, but Mrs. Fitzgerald stood in his way.

"Oh! And if you find we are not quite up to code," she asked sweetly, "then what?"

"Well, then we will have to come back on another day with free smoke detectors for immediate installation," he replied.

"That sounds very nice, my dear," she said, "but I am afraid you have caught us rather on a bad day." She turned and gestured toward Sidney, who felt herself turning pale. "Bad case of the flu."

The policeman glanced up, and Sidney could read the fear of contagion in his eyes. "Right. Thank you, ma'am," was all he said before turning away. The two women watched as he stepped briskly off the porch, down to the front walk and out through the wrought-iron gate, which he closed carefully.

Mrs. Fitzgerald pulled a handkerchief out of a pocket and fanned herself as she leaned against the wall. She looked up at Sidney, who was trying to decide whether to go back into her own apartment or to have a few words. "Cops make me nervous," said Mrs. Fitzgerald. "They remind me of hornets. I know they're beneficial in the scheme of things, but I don't like them buzzing about. It makes me especially uneasy that this character should suddenly show up unannounced and unsummoned. To the best of my knowledge, the cops have not prevented a single assault or robbery in this neighborhood as long as I've been here. The courts turn the thieves loose again even if they get caught. Speaking of hornets, I'm prepared to defend *myself*." She leaned down and picked up a black can from behind the coat rack that stood by the front door. She held it up for Sidney to see. "Hornet spray is the best defense," she said.

Sidney looked puzzled. "How do you mean?" she asked.

Mrs. Fitzgerald chuckled. "Why, hornet spray has a range of twenty feet with about a three-foot-wide spray pattern. Even a nervous female with no prior practice can take down a 250-pound man. At least she can incapacitate him long enough to get away and call for help. And, best of all, it's available almost everywhere: in grocery stores, convenience stores, Walmart, you name it, for less than five dollars! It's a great buy."

After listening silently, Sidney began to cry, softly at first and then in great sobs. Her nose was running. She reached into her pockets for a tissue but couldn't find one. She didn't want to think about needing to defend herself. Suddenly the feeling of panic gripped her again. She had allowed herself to become imprisoned, walled in, locked in, not only in this city and in this house, but in her marriage. Most of all, she was suddenly aware of how afraid she had become. She sat down on the stairs, head in hands, and wept.

When Sidney had exhausted her tears, she looked up. Mrs. Fitzgerald was waiting patiently, watching her with a motherly expression. Looking at her, Sidney suddenly felt safe for the first time in months. "How strange," she thought, "how bizarre and wonderful." She felt safe. She coughed a bit and wiped at her nose, which had started to run again. Mrs. Fitzgerald held up a small packet of tissues between the spindles of the railing. Sidney took it gratefully.

"Could I talk with you?" she asked.

Mrs. Fitzgerald replaced the canister of hornet spray behind the coat rack. "Come on in then, and I'll make you that cup of tea I promised," she said, walking back toward the door of the first-floor apartment. Sidney could hear the Pekingese greeting her, barking loudly. And so, she followed. Her reserve was beginning to reassert itself, but she recalled that she had nothing else to do, and nowhere else to go for the whole day. The thought made her feel rather light and free. She entered a narrow green hallway which had doorways leading into three different rooms. On her left was the living room, separated from the hall by French doors which had tight lacy curtains obscuring the view. She tried to peer in through a small gap between the window frame and curtain. Through this gap, she could see tall bookcases that reached all the way from the floor to the crown moldings.

The dogs had stopped barking and had begun snuffling about in the kitchen. Sidney hesitated. She wasn't sure which way to go and wanted, needed, to sit down. She thought of retreating upstairs. But Mrs. Fitzgerald seemed to reappear magically, like a smiling fairy godmother. She was holding a silver tray with a tea pot, cups, and a jar of honey on it. Pushing open one of the French doors with her foot, she entered the living room, followed closely behind by the hairy little dogs, which jumped onto the sofa and the upholstered chairs. In the middle of the room was a coffee table that was stacked with books. Mrs. Fitzgerald slid a couple of the volumes aside to level the stack, then balanced the tray on top.

All the seats appeared to be occupied by dogs, but as Mrs. Fitzgerald sat down in a red overstuffed chair, the dog in it jumped down just in time. It was a white-and-black creature she referred to as Piggy, which circled several times before settling down in front of the marble hearth. Piggy looked up at Sidney through large, luminous eyes; and Mrs. Fitzgerald smiled down at the animal. "She's my precious!" she said. "Do sit down, dear. Just move the dogs; they'll settle in eventually." Pouring two cups of tea, she added, "Now tell me, what is on your mind?"

Sidney sat down in the nearest chair, facing Mrs. Fitzgerald; but as soon as she had settled herself and seen that the displaced Pekingese had quietly joined one of its fellows on the sofa, she forgot what she had been about to say. The room was too distracting, almost overwhelming. It seemed like a wild museum. Ancient, long-barreled guns with complicated mechanisms hung above the doors and windows. There was a very large oil painting over the fireplace, probably from the Hudson River School, she guessed. African tribal sculptures with bizarre faces stared at her from the mantel. Two dark portraits, an austere-looking lady and an unsmiling gentleman, looked down at her impassively from their old, chipped gilt frames. She spotted a framed collection of arrowheads on another wall. Crowded among the books in the bookcases were mineral specimens, fossils, and the skulls of various animals. A curly sheepskin covered the back of the tattered sofa on which two of the dogs were now snoring softly. A tall-case clock tick-tocked hypnotically.

The silver spoon made a clicking sound in the teacup, and Mrs. Fitzgerald was asking whether she liked a bit of honey in her tea. The sound drew Sidney's attention back to the present and the kindly face of her landlady, but she was becoming nervous again. She folded her hands in her lap to keep them from trembling. She had to talk about the nightmares. She had to. If she didn't, she felt she would explode.

"I can't take it anymore," she blurted out.

Dylan made an early start on his walk across town. The meeting was to take place in the Thurgood Marshall Law Library, which belonged to the University of Maryland School of Law. His repeated checks of the traffic reports during the morning had convinced him that even a cab would be slower than walking. Barricades had been erected, streets had been blocked or made one-way. It almost seemed as if the city authorities were trying to hamper, rather than facilitate, attendance at the ball park. He had already looked at a Google map, and after considering various routes had decided to take Fayette Street most of the way to its intersection with Greene. The alternate possibility of walking west along Pratt street would have had the advantage of taking him past the frigate *Constellation*, which had been on his mind after he smelled the salty air on his way to work. But that route would have been a few blocks out of his way, and he wanted to avoid arriving in a sweat. He was a little surprised to see that the Law School was located on the same block and directly behind Westminster Hall and Graveyard. Across the street stood the University of Maryland's Francis King-Carey Law School, and on the other side the University's Medical Campus and Hospital.

As he walked westward, Dylan marveled at the number of police on duty, directing traffic at every intersection. In spite of their efforts, or perhaps because of them, the streets looked like a parking lot. Drivers were shouting; horns were blowing; and uniformed officers were waving west-bound cars rightward onto north-bound streets. He had no way of knowing that at the same time that he was walking toward the law library, an angry mob was assembling in front of the statue of Babe Ruth. Following the vandalism of the statue, there had been a flurry of tweets and Facebook posts among various groups opposed to the removal of the city's monuments. A coalition calling itself Stand Your Ground had organized a protest around the effigy of the famous slugger, and amazingly had managed to obtain a permit to hold a vigil on Opening Day, with prayers and speeches. A motorcycle club from Harford County had volunteered to link arms in protection of the rally.

By noon, long lines of baseball fans had formed around the side of Camden Yards, hemmed in by chain-link fences. Most wore orange or black. Outside the fence, a noisier and more active crowd was shouting and jeering at a rather frightened-looking corps of miscellaneous types with signs saying, "Preserve our Heritage" and "Baseball is Love" and "America's People, America's Pastime." A large number of policemen were standing by with shields, channeling the demonstrators into a column of twos, through a gauntlet of what later news reports would describe as counter-protesters. These latter wore hooded sweatshirts, mostly gray or black. Many had bandanas or masks covering their faces. A particularly frenetic, thin man in a Guy Fawkes mask was jumping and shouting. Members of the biker club, in black leather and helmets, were trying to interpose themselves between the marchers and the mob. The masked rioters shouted obscenities, chanted "Fascist whites got no rights!" and occasionally lifted their masks to spit. A nauseating stench arose as they threw plastic bags of human excrement at the marchers.

Standing off by himself, a bearded man all in white was holding a Nazi flag. A number of people took his picture, but nobody bothered him. Someone climbed an improvised platform in front of the Babe's statue and began to speak, but no one could hear what he was saying. A police car inched through the crowd, lights flashing, and a loudspeaker announced, "Disperse immediately! The Mayor of the City of Baltimore has declared this an illegal assembly! Disperse immediately!"

The cops sprang into action, pushing the bewildered defenders of the statue back the way they had come, back through the screaming mob. The hooded horde grew bolder, snatching the helmets off the heads of a couple of the bikers and revealing that one of the bikers was a black man. At this discovery, the mob roared with rage, calling him "Uncle Tom" and "house nigger" and trying to drag him to the ground. The man in the Guy Fawkes mask took a swing at him with a baseball bat, but the other bikers closed ranks and pulled him to safety. A stout, helmeted biker stepped forward. "You owe my friend here an apology," he said, and butted Guy Fawkes in the face. The mask cracked down the middle, and its wearer fell backward, bleeding from his nose and mouth.

Suddenly, out of nowhere, men and women in green uniforms and full riot gear stormed through the crowd in a wedge formation, driving the rioters aside and descending on the bikers with truncheons swinging. They began to seize people, seemingly at random, forcing them down on the brick pavement and securing their hands with plastic zip ties. They arrested tweed-coated men with glasses, old ladies in flow-ered dresses and blue-white hair, bikers with pony-tails, and teen-age boys in Orioles jackets. Those who resisted were beaten into submission. All the prisoners were herded into waiting vans bearing a blue-and-green picture of the planet earth with a smiley face on it and the words, "GOOD: Global Outreach Organizing for Diversity." Curiously, the riot police did not arrest a single counter-protester. Meanwhile the long, slow line of fans continued moving into the stadium to drink beer, eat hotdogs, and cheer for the home team.

A few blocks to the north, Dylan arrived at the Law School with fifteen minutes to spare. He found the front en-trance, hung his press pass around his neck, and strode into the building with the confident air of a V.I.P. In the lobby, he was immediately stopped by a uniformed guard. The guard wanted to know the nature of his visit. Dylan told him he was a reporter from the Herald, assigned to attend a meeting be-tween the Westminster Preservation Trust and the organiza-tion "GOOD." He held out his press badge. The guard took it and looked it over carefully before speaking into a little mi-crophone on his chest.

"Reporter from the *Herald*. Okay to send him up?" He cupped a hand over his left ear, listened a moment and nod-ded. Then he looked back at Dylan and said, "Ok, you can go on in; take a left, go up the elevator to the second floor, all the way to the end. Have a nice day." The guard smiled, showing a fine set of gold teeth.

Dylan had no difficulty in finding where the meeting was being held. Several people were standing in the hallway, and he could hear conversations mixed with laughter. Some of the laughter was the chummy and collegial chuckle of insiders. Some was the nervous titter of outsiders. The facial expressions of the people, the hand-shaking and back-clapping among the participants also broke into the same two categories. He stopped outside the door before entering the room, making way for two women who were wearing dark suits and carrying large briefcases. They were engaged in what he supposed was an important private conversation because they stopped talking as they brushed by him.

He found a place to stand in the back, next to a long table that held urns of coffee and bowls filled with condiments: packets of real and artificial sugars, creamers, and honey. Sealed containers of fruit juice rested on a bed of crushed ice. Porcelain coffee cups and little plated silver spoons flanked a stack of white paper napkins stamped with the University of Maryland insignia. There were also plates of donuts and bagels with cream cheese and salmon spreads. Trying to be inconspicuous, he crammed a white powdered confection into his mouth. In his haste to get downtown, he had forgotten to eat his lunch. He regretted it now, staring at the other goodies that lay on the table. Unsure whether guest reporters were supposed to partake, but reasoning that his hunger pangs might interfere with the discharge of his journalistic duty, he downed a cup of orange juice. Then he heaped some salmon spread on a bagel.

Soon others came into the room, finding places around the conference table. Someone had carefully orchestrated this event. There were name tags at each place, and each participant received a faux-leather folder containing a yellow legal pad. Pens and bottles of spring water had been laid out like place settings at a formal dinner. All the men wore dark suits and ties. He felt rather shabby and insignificant now in his polo shirt and tan windbreaker. He had no assigned place at the table. He picked nervously at the clear plastic holder of his press pass. A fast-walking young woman handed him a fact sheet.

The controversial business before the University was the selling of Westminster Hall and Graveyard. The purchaser was G.O.O.D., Global Outreach Organizing for Diversity. It was the understanding of the University that GOOD wanted the site for the construction of a significant building. This building or complex of buildings would make quite a noticeable addition to the skyline of Baltimore, and more so to the University of Maryland campus. The staff was to be enormous, their salaries huge, and their mission global. GOOD anticipated that over 10,000 new jobs would be added to the downtown workforce within two to four years.

From the murmurings round the table, Dylan gathered that most of the attendees from the University did not know at first that there was any question about the sale of Westminster Hall. They knew of course from their agenda sheet that item Ten was, "Disposition of University Property," but that or something similar appeared at almost every meeting, and they were not very interested. On the other hand, they did notice that item One was "Questions about Westminster Hall and Graveyard." A stout black woman was introduced first, Dr. Olivia Brown, president of the Westminster Preservation Trust, Inc. She had several letters to read to those in attendance.

The first was from the Maryland Historical Society about its "concern for the conservation of the interior of Westminster Hall and the proper presentation of detailed information about the buried remains at this important historical site."

"It would be wiser," Dr. Brown suggested, "for the Historical Society to focus on the deteriorating condition of the property as a whole." She went on to say that the brick piers supporting the church building were in dubious condition with deteriorating mortar. She held up a grainy photograph of something that could have been a block of cheese and stated that unfortunately the bricks placed below grade were not much better than unfired clay and were resting on unstable, water-soaked muck. What was needed was a more thorough assessment, and the MHS should take "a broader view concerning disposition of antiquities that comprised the Westminster Hall and Graveyard." She thanked the representatives of GOOD for funding the engineering analysis that had brought these concerns to light.

There was another letter, from the Society of Spiritual Science, asking permission to investigate reported "mysterious phenomena" within the graveyard at Westminster. Dr. Brown gave the audience a knowing smirk and a raised eyebrow. A quiet chuckle ran through the assembly

A third letter was from a Mrs. Hausman, who reported bringing a Cub Scout den on a Halloween tour to see the "catacomb," as she called it, and finding to her horror that there was "a small coffin floating in filthy water inside an open grave." Dr. Brown rolled her eyes at this account, and a general murmur of incredulity seemed to confirm her judgment. A brief discussion followed, and a resolution was passed instructing Dr. Brown to write appropriately dismissive letters. The meeting moved forward to the next order of business.

Then came a new voice from a different part of the room. Dr. Armand Black had risen. He fully agreed that the condition of the property in all of its complexity should be taken into full consideration by the University and its agents, deferring of course to the Preservation Trust. The mission of the University and the Trust were the paramount considerations, and interference from amateur preservationists and ghost hunters had no place in the discussion.

"I speak, be it understood, as a consultant historian, and it is my hope that I may be seen as a good-will ambassador. I am here in my capacity as a consultant for GOOD, and I am most desirous of doing all I can to promote a better understanding of the importance of maintaining the integrity of Westminster Hall and its legendary graveyard." He rested his hand on a stack of yellowed documents and dingy leather-bound books. "Mind you, I defer to legal counsel for all parties with respect to the detailed questions that necessarily attend upon a matter of such magnitude, but for my own part, I welcome the opportunity to facilitate the necessary structural and environmental surveys and review of all relevant easements and titles, prior to the consummation of any sale."

Then Black went on to read from a letter from the Secretary of the governing board of GOOD.

As a member of the board of directors of Global Outreach Organizing for Diversity, I'm personally thrilled to be a part of an organization that has truly embraced the core values that drive Baltimore's community con-

servation movement. By boldly advancing historic conservation efforts throughout the city of Baltimore and the state of Maryland, there is a unique opportunity to embrace diverse people and communities that have traditionally not been part of historic conservation. It's truly inspiring that so many organizations like the University of Maryland have fully embraced this opportunity with commitment, innovation and pure passion. I believe that GOOD's extraordinary community conservation work will continue to broaden and strengthen historic conservation, elevate its relevancy and have a lasting positive impact for future generations."

Almost at once, the Chief Financial Officer of the University was on his feet. He welcomed Dr. Black's helpful comments and expressed his grave concern about "the University's liabilities with regard to what, though a beloved if not particularly distinguished piece of Victorian-era kitsch," (quiet giggles came from several of the attendees) "has unfortunately reached what I think might be characterized as the 'high-maintenance' or 'intensive care' stage of its existence. Do you concur, Dr. Black?"

Black smiled agreeably. "As you all know," he said, "the church was built on brick pilings for the express purpose of stabilizing the property, which was in the process of sliding down the hill toward the Jones Falls. Who knows; but for those long-ago efforts, the contents of the graves might have ended up floating around in Baltimore Harbor. Alas, the little works of humankind are no match for the mighty forces of time and water. Oh, yes, water! I regret to confirm that the floating casket story in the letter Dr. Brown just presented is only too true! Now, I do not hold myself out as a builder or a financial expert, but my initial research suggests that it might almost be cheaper to move the whole church than to put it right."

The room erupted with protests and shouted questions. After several minutes, Dr. Brown restored order. Reluctantly, and with endearing modesty, Dr. Black gave tentative responses to a multitude of questions from those present, including the amount required to rebuild the brick piers, install modern drains, and reline the crypts. Of course, he could not guarantee, no one could, that additional structural damage might not result from the foundation work. He hesitated before giving a possible total figure for the restoration, and the projected cost brought many gasps from the assembled group.

Noisy arguments broke out all around the table. Someone was shouting, "Didn' I tell you? Didn' I tell you?" A very old man rose unsteadily and banged his cane on the table. "Pack of lies!" he wheezed. "Who are these people?" But no one seemed to hear him. When order was again restored, the group agreed to table the matter pending further investigation.

The next item for discussion was about ongoing correspondence between Global Outreach Organizing for Diversity (GOOD) and the University of Maryland's medical school. Apparently, the medical school had pledged full cooperation and support to partner with and share critical research between the school and GOOD's own private biomedical engineering projects. There were new and exciting possibilities at stake. New initiatives were under way relating to neurological science, and the possibility of "optimizing the human brain." The word "Singularity" came up repeatedly.

A man with a blotchy, bald head was saying, "This combined research commitment holds promise not only for human achievement but for the elimination of conflict, both here and all around the world." He went on in a monotone, inviting the audience to imagine a world without ignorance, hate, fear, hunger, disease, inequality, and on and on. There seemed to be nothing that this new "partnership" would not cure. Self-organizing nanoparticles were well on their way; three-dimensional printing of human organs was already a reality; implanted microcomputer chips would be as much a necessity as smart phones.

The room was uncomfortably warm. People were shifting in their seats and looking at their watches. Even though he was standing up, Dylan was having a hard time staying awake. He was beginning to wonder how he could possibly write anything but a snoozer about these technical and financial concerns about some old building, and all this pie-in-the-sky about remaking the human race. Now other people were speaking, the assistant counsel for this and the coordinator for that. It was becoming harder and harder to sort out who spoke for which organization. Someone with a very thick foreign accent read a very long mission statement of some sort. The whole boring scene seemed to recede into the distance. Dylan had begun by feeling like a non-member eavesdropping on an exciting meeting of a private club. Now he felt more like a Martian watching a small-town parade through a telescope.

Suddenly, people were standing up. Several were approaching the refreshment table. The old man with the cane was shaking his head and muttering as he hobbled out into the hall. Dylan looked at his copy of the agenda. The next item was "BREAK."

Dylan wasn't sure what to do now, so he remained standing at his place near the refreshments. Nonchalantly opening a bottle of Italian spring water, he took a sip and stood back to allow the others to reach the goodies. Some ignored him completely. Others gave a curt nod as they passed. A pretty girl in a navy-blue suit with a short skirt paused and gave him a shy smile. Her badge said "Intern." It hung just below the top of her low-cut blouse. Dylan did not have time to register her name. It was a long name, and he was afraid that too long a glance in that direction might be misinterpreted. Just as he was formulating a question about the relationship between the Trust and the University, the woman behind her gave him an icy look and ordered the intern to come along.

Dylan could feel his face turning red. Then someone behind him said, "Ahem." Suddenly assailed by visions of being accused of sexual harassment on his first big assignment, he turned around. Standing before him was a trim, tidy man of middle age, with jet-black hair and a charcoal gray suit. The man reached out and took hold of Dylan's press pass, which he scrutinized as if it were a rare insect. In the awkward silence, Dylan saw that the man was none other than Dr. Armand Black. Up close, he had a very authoritative, professorial presence, but there was something disconcerting about him too, something restless, even shifty.

"Mr. Greene! Well, well! I do believe you're the most important person at this gathering. I'm sure it hasn't escaped your notice that you are the only representative of the news media in attendance. This must seem very dull stuff to a hard-working reporter for a great metropolitan newspaper."

"Dull? Oh, not at all!" lied Dylan, who had still not come up with any angle that might lend interest to the article that he would have to write.

"You're not a Baltimorean," remarked Black with such assurance that Dylan wondered how he could be so certain. The statement hung in the air between them. Black seemed to be waiting for a reply.

"Sometimes they let in Midwesterners. I guess they had to fill a quota," Dylan replied, immediately wondering whether he had been too flippant with this important person and, worse, whether the "quota" quip would be interpreted as a subtle dig against affirmative action. He was relieved when Black smiled in reply. At least his mouth smiled, and dimples appeared in his cheeks; but his eyes darted to left and right before fixing themselves again on Dylan.

"You'll want to stick around. The really interesting part comes in Act Two. After the meeting, you can tell me if I was right." Giving Dylan a pat on the back, he walked out into the hall and greeted a group of trustees. His laughter carried back into the conference room. It was a deep, sonorous laugh, and the trustees were laughing along with him.

The efficient woman with the information packets was blinking the room lights. After some coughing and rustling of papers, the participants returned to their assigned seats. Three seats were empty now. The geezer with the cane and a couple of others had apparently huffed off.

The next order of business was about the long correspondence between the University of Maryland and GOOD regarding the proposed participation of GOOD in the University's Francis King-Carey School of Law. One of the rather severe-looking women with brief cases summarized the negotiations to date. It appeared that the University had expressed qualified support for this proposal, which involved complicated alterations to the University's charter and a number of by-agreements concerning employment contracts, leases, reassignment of office space and job titles, and subsidiary articles of understanding with respect to authority for appointments, disbursement of funds, and recruitment of international scholars. There was a general framework in place for protection of intellectual property relating to the biomedical and cyber-research divisions that would interface with the School of Medicine. There was a large, no, a *very* large sum of money that could be made available to the University for the construction of a proposed Global Justice Tower to house the proposed new International Social Justice Institute. The legal teams were only days away from ironing out the last little wrinkles.

There was just one problem: an insufficiency of available space. A long discussion followed, with maps and satellite images projected on a big screen at one end of the room. Someone tried to close the blinds, but there was still a bit too much light in the room to make out all the details. A spokesperson from the Mayor's office rose to speak on behalf of the Mayor and City Council to express grave concern about westward expansion of the campus and "gentrification" of adjacent neighborhoods. She read from a piece of paper.

"We as members of a community of color need to speak up. Gentrification is a form of institutional racism directed against people of African/Indigenous descent. It is a manifestation of the apparatus of neo-colonialism under control of white-dominated financial institutions determined to displace melanated beings from parts of the city that are suffering economically. Thank you."

A period of throat-clearing and paper-rustling followed.

Dr. Brown's financial report for the Preservation Trust, Inc. was next on the agenda. Operating expenses were increasing as a result of unexpected maintenance and code-compliance costs. Revenues from event rentals of the church building had been disappointing. Prospective renters who had chosen to go elsewhere gave "difficult parking" as their main reason for selecting other venues. Dr. Brown explained that she interpreted this objection as a coded reference to fear of violent crime. Grants for historic preservation were expected to be less available as a result of cut-backs by the debt-laden

state and federal governments. Tax incentives for private donors had dropped off, possibly because the older donors were
dying, or possibly as a result of changes to the tax code.

She went on: "It's difficult to promote a graveyard to the
American Public despite the fact that Edgar Allan Poe
happens to be buried there. Millennials are turned off by re-
minders of death at a wedding venue. Westminster Hall and
its cemetery comprise some of the most historically important
ground on the University's campus. Unfortunately, the task
of protecting, conserving and restoring the Hall and the
graveyard has become increasingly problematic. It is the
opinion of the board of the Preservation Trust that additional
funding is urgently needed if the Trust is to continue its important work."

A murmur arose as Dr. Brown resumed her seat and introduced the next speaker. He was a small gray man in a gray
suit. Even when he stood and began speaking, some of the
committee looked around in surprise. No one had noticed him
until that moment. He had wispy gray hair that occasionally
fell across his face as he talked, and a pair of gray reading
glasses that gradually slid down his thin nose as if they were
trying to land on his thin mustache. His movements to replace
the hairs and the glasses were exceptionally distracting. In a
thin, wavering voice, he said, "My name is, um, Gifford
Wheedler, and as assistant counsel to the advisory committee

of, um, the central directorate, I bring you greetings and, um, what I hope will be good news, from the Global Outreach. There is a solution to all of the, um, difficulties that have been raised at today's meeting."

A long pause followed as he rummaged in a brown-paper shopping bag and withdrew a sheaf of papers, which slipped out of his thin hands and spilled in every direction. Mr. Wheedler made curious mumbling noises as he carefully gathered and reorganized the papers. There was no other sound in the room.

"I have to apologize for the quality of the, um, visual aids, but this" he held up a small map, looked at it vaguely, then turned it over, then flipped it around so that the people across the table could almost see it. "This is a conceptual diagram, albeit not, um, you know, exactly to scale, showing the arrangement of buildings on the campus. Available lots are colored in green, unavailable lots in red, and possibly available lots in amber. As you can see, there is no green on the map within a reasonable radius of the law school. There is, um, one amber area in the same block as the Thurgood Marshall Law Library."

Dr. Brown rose immediately. "*That* is the site of the Westminster Church and Graveyard!" she gasped.

Mr. Wheedler smiled as if this were exactly the point. "Oh, yes, so you see how we can solve all our little problems at once. Global Outreach is willing (and here I can speak on behalf of the central directorate) to fund the relocation of the historic church and graves to a beautiful corner of Druid Ridge Cemetery in Pikesville, where there will be no shortage of parking, and the church will overlook a lake. And, um, generous stipends have been voted to sustain the endowment of the Trust and to fund an appropriate, um, salary for its management. This sort of, um, move is easily accomplished. And all structural issues would obviously be addressed. Then the amber area will be available for construction of the Global Justice Tower."

He abruptly stopped speaking and looked around the room. "I interpret your silence to mean that you are thinking the same thing I'm thinking: Only a heartless, um, monster or something would stand in the way of such a plan to save a Baltimore landmark and promote global equity."

Someone fumed, "So you're preemptively trying to silence opposition by name-calling! And what exactly is global equity?"

But several people merely shook their heads at such old-fashioned thinking. Animated conversations blended into a general buzz of satisfaction with the "brilliant proposal" by GOOD. Motions were made, seconded, and approved. The committee would recommend immediate coordination of efforts between GOOD and the University.

As the meeting broke up, Dylan found that he was again speaking with Armand Black, who addressed him with a knowing smile. "Well, was I right?"

"I guess you were!" Dylan replied.

"Before you turn in your story, you might want a little on background?" suggested Black. "I've made a dinner reservation in Little Italy if you'd like to come along."

Chapter 5

Sidney departed the house sometime around noon. She had left her watch in the apartment, and the clock on her car's instrument panel had stopped working; but it felt like noon because the empty feeling in her stomach reminded her that she had forgotten to eat breakfast, what with the peculiar visit by the snoopy policeman and then her disturbing conversation with her landlady. She shuddered as she drove north towards the beltway and remembered what Mrs. Fitzgerald had told her. "I think your nightmares represent a psychic experience, not a mental breakdown."

The interview had begun normally enough. After they had both had a few sips of tea, Sidney had described her frightening dreams, including parts that she hadn't shared with Dylan, about a ghoulish old man in a motorized wheelchair who devoured corpses. Sometimes he was tiny, like a maggot inside a sarcophagus. Then he would be a giant, lifting up a church, always the same church, *that* church, to get at the graves beneath it. And somehow this ghoul knew she was watching him! Mrs. Fitzgerald had nodded as if the wild visions all made perfect sense, then picked up a little purple velvet bag that lay among the clutter on the coffee table. She undid the drawstring, opened the bag, and took out a deck of ornate cards. Sidney was puzzled.

"What's this?" she asked, wondering whether the older woman had decided she was a lunatic who need to be humored with some diversion.

Mrs. Fitzgerald replied with a question. "Would you like me to read your cards?"

"You mean like a gypsy fortune teller?" Sidney replied, then remembered too late that "gypsy" was one of those insensitive words they had told her to avoid in one of her mandatory training sessions at the college.

"This is a Tarot deck, and I'm actually rather good at reading the future for those who are not certain about what direction to take. And, since you seem at a crossroads of sorts, I thought a reading might shed some light upon your path." Mrs. Fitzgerald sat back in her overstuffed chair and waited for Sidney to respond.

"I'm not sure if I believe in that kind of stuff," Sidney said.

"What kind of stuff?" Mrs. Fitzgerald asked.

"Oh, you know, hocus pocus, and pull a bunny out of a hat sort of thing."

This last statement amused Mrs. Fitzgerald, and she started to laugh, and the dogs looked up from their various positions on the furniture and began to yip. The one she referred to as Piggy waged her tail and leapt to her feet, whining. Mrs. Fitzgerald looked down at the dog, and some communication seemed to pass between them because Piggy appeared satisfied and picked a spot nearby to lie down again. Mrs. Fitzgerald turned back to Sidney and explained, "I just told her to lie down, and that we would take a nice little walk later."

This clarification only served to make Sidney more uneasy. Did the landlady talk to animals too? Was she some kind of mind reader? Nonsense.

"Now, dear, I am going to do a spread of the cards and hope that it will give us some clarity about your dreams and maybe provide some guidance for you." She shuffled the cards and began laying them out in a pattern that looked like a cross. Some cards showed pictures of kings and queens. One had a man hanging upside down from a tree. Another depicted a couple holding hands and standing beneath a rainbow.

After some time examining the cards, and after several hum's and ah-ha's, Mrs. Fitzgerald looked up at Sidney. "My dear, you are definitely standing at a crossroads and fearful of which direction to take. You have been in this place for far too long. The moment of decision is at hand; there can be no stopping or waiting. If you do nothing, then events will sweep you along the dark path, and darkness will prevail. And I am getting the distinct impression that you have some degree of psychic ability of your own, with access to critical information of interest to certain groups of individuals, some of whom will want to use this information for evil."

Sidney jumped up. "How can you tell me such crazy nonsense?" she demanded angrily. "I wasn't born yesterday, you know. I've read the phony horoscopes in the papers and the hokey messages inside fortune cookies. They all depend on universal experiences and confirmation bias."

Mrs. Fitzgerald folded her hands in her lap. "That's true," she said.

"And I'll tell you another thing…" began Sidney. "What did you say?"

"I said that's true. The world is full of tricksters who profit from credulity and the power of suggestion. But what do *you* really think? You didn't come to me because you believed you were having ordinary dreams."

Sidney sat down again.

"I think you need to pay a visit to a close friend of mine," Mrs. Fitzgerald said. "Her name is Wanda. She's very good with this sort of problem; and she's a minister and a healer besides. She lives about an hour from here, in a place called Rising Sun. Let me give her a call and see if she can't see you today."

"To tell you the truth, I'd be willing to eat out of garbage cans in New York City if I thought it might help me," Sidney said.

"Ugh! Now that *would* be drastic, and I don't think it would do anything to help you, dear!" Mrs. Fitzgerald said.

"All right, ok then, I'll give it a try," Sidney said. I feel as if I'm ready to jump out of my skin, and I took the whole day off, so I guess a drive sounds pretty good." And so, after her landlady had made a quick phone call and jotted down some directions, Sidney began driving north, then east, then north again, toward Rising Sun.

Armand Black had a chauffeured car waiting. He and Dylan climbed into the spacious back seat while Gifford Wheedler scrunched into the front seat next to the driver. There were crunching and mumbling noises as the assistant counsel tucked his paper bags into the space between the floor and the dashboard. As the car pulled away from the curb, Dylan was surprised to see that there was almost no traffic. Speeding eastward on Baltimore Street, he suddenly saw why: city police and green-uniformed officers from GOOD had blocked most of the intersections. The men and women in green wore white helmets with "PEACE" in green letters.

Dylan smiled involuntarily.

"What's so funny?" asked Black.

Startled that the older man had been watching him so closely, Dylan stammered, "Oh, well, I was just thinking, 'GOOD cop, bad cop.'"

Armand Black laughed his hearty laugh. "Very true, that! The Freddie Gray case set them up for a hostile takeover, didn't it? Can't justify lifting a consent decree without a plan for correction, can we? What's a few cars and buildings burned if social justice moves forward, eh?"

Dylan was relieved at first that Black had appreciated his witticism, but his relief immediately gave way to uneasiness. He knew that he was under scrutiny. Fortunately, he thought he agreed in general with the direction that the conversation was taking. "No omelet without eggs," he ventured.

He was rewarded with another deep laugh from the historian. "Quite so, quite so. Still, I wonder sometimes whether these, shall we say, spontaneous demonstrations are being managed carefully enough." This remark seemed to be directed toward Wheedler, who turned around in his seat.

"If you want to know whether the mix of professionals was right, just look at what actually happened. It was only, um, expendable items that burned. The non-professionals, the extras if you will, were naturally drawn from the, um, minority population (actually the majority in the city if one wishes to be technically accurate, which of course I wish to be), and they can be, um, excitable."

"That's where we risk losing control of the narrative," retorted Black.

"Now, now, Armand. A good workman never blames his tools. Besides, the narrative is what folks like young Dylan here say it is."

"I hope you like Italian food," said Black, elbowing Dylan in the ribs. "Did you bring an appetite?"

The restaurant was about half full. The diners seemed on edge. There were murmurings about a riot at the ballpark. A dark-haired hostess with full lips and a tight black dress led the three to a table in the back of the place. She handed out menus and a wine list. A young lady appeared in a pressed white blouse and black skirt and offered to take drink orders.

The waitress seemed quite taken with Dr. Black. Indeed, she spoke to him as if he were the only one at the table. He stared deep into her brown eyes and said, "We'll start with a bottle of wine. How about the Rosso di Montalcino?" He rolled the words out with an impeccable Tuscan accent and a little flourish of his right hand. Looking at Dylan with raised eyebrows, he added, "Unless you'd prefer something different?"

Dylan had been planning to ask for a beer, but instead he only smiled and shook his head. "I think I'll just go wash my hands, if you'll excuse me." Following the signs, he made his way to the restroom. He found it quaint that the signs still said Ladies and Gentlemen. He wondered when the folks in this backward ethnic enclave would get in step with the times. Didn't they know that binary gender-specific bathrooms do irreparable psychological damage to persons of alternative or fluid gender identity? And Ladies? Gentlemen? How elitist! He nevertheless stepped into the room of his own chosen gender and latched the door. After using the facilities, he took out his cell phone to call Sidney. When the call went directly to her voice mail, he sent a text instead, the same one he had used many times before: **Home late, Important dinner, XX D**, before returning to the table.

Black and Wheedler had already begun sipping their wine and eating crusty bread dipped in olive oil. "An intimate chat with the Mrs., eh?" Black asked.

Dylan nodded. "Yes, sir," he replied.

"Mm. Young love. Nothing like it."

This comment seemed to switch on some circuit in Mr. Wheedler, who spoke around and through the wad of bread in his mouth. "Ah, the delights and benefits of connubial bliss! All the best research suggests that communication coupled with conflict resolution skills is a prerequisite to having a happy relationship. Don't you find it so?" He smiled confidentially at Dylan. Without waiting for a reply, he went on.

"Let me elaborate," he said. "Our Sociology Department's key focus at GOOD is the development of programs of conflict resolution, and naturally conflict resolution begins at home.

"Restaurant service can be analogized with marriage." He said, sweeping his arms across the table for emphasis. The gesture upset Wheedler's wine glass, and a dark red wave leapt across the table cloth and into Dylan's lap. Wheedler appeared not to notice. "At GOOD, our data has shown that when a spouse serves the other unselfishly and uninhibitedly (mind you, getting to this stage in any relationship takes a great deal of effort and commitment) it's, um, the same as what's at the heart of the work that goes into making a workplace and by extension family and community life successful. The attitude we are looking for can be summed up in one statement: I am a servant to my work!

"Resistance usually comes from a place of misguided ego. What GOOD looks for in its, um, shall I say associates, is that one's own pride and sense of entitlement are, um, subsumed by a devotion to the larger group. It usually takes coaching and behavioral management along with constant feed-back and support, but the individual soon yields up their individual will, giving fully according to their ability, and of course the collective reciprocates in an appropriate fashion."

Dylan looked at his lap. Black had already gestured to the waitress, who took away the soaked napkin and hurried back with a handful of wet towels, with which she began wiping the front of Dylan's shirt. The other diners were turning to look at him. As awkward as he felt, he was relieved not to have to make an immediate reply to Mr. Wheedler, whose little speech had left him at a loss. With a fresh napkin settled in his lap, he took a sip of wine. Both of his companions were regarding him intently, apparently awaiting an answer.

"Why are you telling me all this?" he finally asked.

The little gray man looked at his empty wine glass with perplexity. It had, after all, been full when he began speaking. Then he pursed his thin lips and said, "Abandoning the ego, and such, um, divisive, archaic notions as objective truth, personal honor, religious rules and commandments, and so forth, and embracing the good of all, that is the essence of true service to humanity, and beyond humanity, to the planet itself! Those who learn to serve will be in a much better place for recognition and advancement." He winked. "You, um, if I may say so without undue presumption, seem like a young man who would appreciate an opportunity to move events, to make a difference in the world on a global scale, and to live life at a level beyond anything you could have imagined."

"Is this some kind of a job-offer?" asked Dylan. His shirt front was chilly from the waitress's application of wet towels, and he was becoming impatient.

The faces of his two companions took on an expression between embarrassment and shock, as if he had blown his nose on the linen napkin or told an ethnic joke.

"I believe my colleague was speaking in generalities," replied Black after an awkward pause. "We brought you along this evening so that you could get a bit of background on GOOD. You are going to write a story tomorrow about our development plans and our partnership with the University, aren't you?"

"Yes, absolutely. I must have misunderstood. So, uh, if I may, let me ask you a few questions that our readers would like answered. Did I understand correctly that the whole church and cemetery are going to be moved out to the county to make room for a big new building?"

Wheedler beamed. "Oh, my, my, *big* is barely adequate to describe the scope and scale of this project. Dare I say that Baltimore could rival Brussels or The Hague as a center of international legal scholarship and, um, leadership? Great things are in motion here."

"So, the antique church building will be completely reconstructed? Or do they move it in sections? How does that work, and who will do the moving?"

Wheedler tapped his eyeglasses on the table and squinted. "I'm afraid those are matters outside my area of expertise, but as you know, this sort of thing is done all the time."

"And who is paying for all of this moving and construction?"

"My office can forward you a summary of the financing, a broad-brush portrait, as it were. All subject to revision and so forth."

"Shall we order?" suggested Dr. Black.

The meal proceeded without Dylan obtaining any satisfactory answers to specific questions about details of the project or, for that matter, about the Global Outreach Organizing for Diversity, beyond the sort of stuff that he could have extracted from the organization's on-line mission statement. World peace. Conflict management. Equality of all peoples. Saving the environment. Anti-racism. Anti-fascism. Equity. It all sounded about right to him, but it was vague. He would have to write a generally up-beat report. Obviously, the correct intentions were there.

The food was excellent, and the second and third bottles of wine were even better than the first. Armand Black proved to be a master of pleasant small talk. When the car halted to deposit Dylan in front of the *Herald's* office building, Black handed him a business card. "I sense that your questions about our organization were not answered as fully as you might have liked," he said with a smile. "What say I take you out to our regional headquarters on Sunday? Eh? Give me a call."

———————————

Sidney decided to ignore her GPS navigation, which would have taken her up the hectic Interstate 95 for many miles before the exit to Rising Sun. Instead, she followed the handwritten directions Mrs. Fitzgerald had given her. This route looked as if it would be easier on her frayed nerves. She hated thruways, where everyone seemed to be driving too fast and the scenery was nondescript. Concrete barriers and long stretches of roadway that could be anywhere or nowhere made her want to scream. She drove around the top of 695, known to locals as the Beltway, exited at White Marsh Boulevard, and then headed north on Route 1. As she drove along, she was delighted to find that this route took her through small hamlets and farming country. She began to drive leisurely, rolling down her window to let the fresh air clear her mind.

There were gently rolling hills and small farms nestled among groves of old cedars and black-locust trees. She drove by two different horse farms; the first was surrounded by white fences, grazing horses, and green fields. The second had a mansion located on a hill-top, with what she imagined must be a magnificent view. She was becoming more relaxed as she drove, so much so that she didn't even care that Route 1 took her through the town of Belair with its numerous traffic lights. She was surprised to find that she was even charmed by the garish strip malls advertising everything from nail salons and pizza joints to batteries and auto parts.

Fairly soon she was out in the countryside again, and the road was bumpier, dipping and winding through places that had dignified-looking homes and well-tended lawns. The barns looked freshly painted. She smiled, remembering how nice it used to be to live in a rural village, where there was peace and quiet, not the ever-present police sirens of Baltimore.

Sidney slowed down as the road crossed over Conowingo Dam, which had been built just under a century ago to harness the electric generating power of the mighty Susquehanna River. She glanced over the guard rail and gripped the steering wheel more tightly. It was a long way down. Far below, she saw large boulders and foaming white water. Bald eagles were soaring above the rapids, almost at eye level with her! The roadway seemed barely wide enough for two cars to pass each other. "Other people have crossed in safety," she told herself. "So can I." Once across, she pulled off the road and checked her written directions again because Mrs. Fitzgerald had told her to begin looking for the road to Wanda's place shortly after crossing the river and to watch closely because it was easy to miss the turn.

But there it was, the road sign on the left, a short way past Bank of America. She turned onto

Rolandsville Road. Not much farther now! After a couple of miles, she was to turn right into Wanda's driveway. There were no markings or signs. Wanda's drive was apparently either a private road or one of the old, unpaved secondary roads. At the entrance, there was supposed to be a small outbuilding with weathered red trim. She didn't see a mailbox but turned anyway and drove almost half a mile before glimpsing an old farmhouse, several outbuildings, and a large pond surrounded by willow trees. The willow wands were beginning to turn green. They waved in the breeze, and their tips brushed the surface of the pond.

The house was of red brick. Flagstone steps led down from the driveway to a screened-in back porch. Perennial flower beds and terraced herb gardens flanked the steps on both sides. Sidney imagined that she could smell their fragrance even before she got out of her car. She recognized the leaves of thyme, rosemary, and sage, all of which had survived the winter. A few early spring flowers were just starting to bloom. She stepped out of the car and looked around. There were no sounds except birds singing in the bushes and frogs croaking in the pond nearby. Before she could worry about what to do next, she saw that someone was coming out to greet her, a middle-aged woman in bib overalls, her auburn hair in a long braid down her back. She was barefoot. Sidney looked down at her own clothes: sensible shoes with a white shirt over khaki pants: had she over-dressed? She felt out of place, perhaps even somehow out of time, and wanted to get back into her car again.

The woman, who seemed cheerfully oblivious to Sidney's anxiety, took the steps two at a time. She was trim and athletic, with a sun-tanned complexion. She wiped her hands on the sides of her pants and introduced herself. "Hey," she said, "I'm Linda, and I was informed that someone by the name of Sidney was paying us a visit this afternoon. I assume that's you?" Without waiting for a reply, she turned and skipped back down the steps and opened the door to the porch. Not looking back to see if her guest had followed, she went in. "So, don't just stand there," she yelled back. "We haven't got all day!" Sidney followed, gingerly holding on to the wooden railing. She thought the flagstones seemed better suited to bare feet than to shoes with heels.

"Take a seat," Linda said, and pointed to a table at one end of the porch with several comfortable-looking chairs. From that part of the porch, Sidney had a good view of the pond, where the frogs were croaking louder than before, so much so that the sound was almost deafening.

"Are the frogs always so loud?" Sidney asked.

Linda smiled. "Don't mind them, they're only announcing that someone new has arrived."

"What do you mean?"

"Well, the frogs croak to let any intruder know that they are here and in force. What the frogs are actually saying is, 'Here I am! Here I am! Here we are! Beware, for we are many!'"

"Oh," was the only thing Sidney could think of to say. She looked out at the pond and wondered what kind of people have watch frogs.

"Wanda is with another client right now, but please sit here and wait. I think she will be done soon. Would you like a cup of tea?" Linda asked.

"No thanks," Sidney said, "I've had enough tea today." She remembered how Mrs. Fitzgerald had refilled her tea cup several times that morning. She didn't think she could manage another drop.

"I'll just wait."

Suddenly the frogs stopped croaking. Sidney thought maybe they had figured out that she meant them no harm. All she wanted to do was talk to somebody. Maybe Wanda would help her to make sense of the dreams she'd been having.

Within the house, Sidney could hear voices and the clanging of pots and pans. A delicious smell wafted onto the porch where she was sitting. It reminded her of dinner time at her grandmother's house when she was a child, and she remembered how hungry she was. Damn it. She should have come better prepared and not hungry. She loathed being beholden to anyone, especially strangers. She refused to ask for something to eat and was torn between hoping that someone would invite her to join them at the table and dreading to incur an obligation.

Before long, Linda appeared at the ancient Dutch door leading to the interior of the farmhouse. She took a bite from what looked like a fried chicken leg, wiped her mouth on the sleeve of her shirt and, because her mouth was quite full, waved to Sidney to come inside. Once inside, Linda led her through a dark hallway. It was some sort of "mud room," or perhaps a pantry, but Sidney couldn't tell which. There was a tall coat rack on one side that held some jackets, and there was a built-in cupboard on the other side that was stacked with dishes and mason jars filled with canned vegetables. From the hallway, Sidney could see into the next room, which looked like a large dining area. Upon entering, she saw that there was a small kitchen on her left. On her right, there was a long farm table in the middle of the room, with a fire place to one side. In the kitchen, a man was chopping vegetables and paid no attention to her. A kettle was simmering on the stove. It must be soup, Sidney thought. Her stomach began to growl again.

Linda turned around and smiled at Sidney, chicken leg still in hand, using it to point towards another doorway. "Wanda's in there," she said.

Sidney stood still, not quite sure what to do next. Did she just go in? Wasn't she supposed to be introduced or something?

"Go on," Linda said. "She's waiting for you."

Sidney crossed the dining room, making her way around the long table, and went into another hallway where a staircase led to the second floor of the house. Ahead of her was another doorway. She now looked into a bright, sunny sitting room. It was warm and inviting. She went in.

In a big Victorian armchair with dark wood and claw feet, there was an older woman who sat with her hands folded in her lap. "I am Wanda, and you must be Sidney," she said. "Come in and sit down." Wanda patted an adjacent chair and said, "Sit right here so I can see you." She smiled benignly.

Sidney sat down. She dropped her purse on the floor beside her and waited for Wanda to do something. She sat for what seemed like an eternity; but in reality, it couldn't have been more than a couple of minutes. Nonetheless it afforded Sidney a chance to take a better look at Wanda.

Mrs. Fitzgerald had said that this person was a spiritual healer, but she certainly did not look anything like what Sidney imagined a healer should look like. Why wasn't she wearing some kind of Asian garb, perhaps a turban or head scarf or hoop earrings? Where was the crystal ball? Wanda looked more like some of the homeless people she had seen begging for money on the street corners of Baltimore, although she wasn't as bedraggled as they were. She had long black hair, streaked with white. It was pulled back into a ratty-looking pony tail. A feather, possibly an owl feather, was tucked into her hair. She had a prominent nose and rather coarse features. And she was fat. Sidney remembered her recent mandatory training session on "Body Shaming" and tried to erase that thought. But it was difficult when the person in question was stuffed into a faded blue sweat shirt and dark pants that didn't quite button at the top. And she was wearing sneakers, not that there was anything wrong with *that.*

But a strange thing was beginning to happen as Sidney stared into the eyes of this ungainly woman. A wonderful essence began filling the room. It smelled like roses; only there weren't any flowers of any kind there. She felt as if she was being permeated with warmth, but better than that. She felt like a beloved child who was visiting her grandmother for the first time after a long absence. Sidney didn't know what to say. She was feeling so peaceful that she had quite forgotten why she had come there in the first place.

Wanda cleared her throat and coughed into a handkerchief she pulled from her shirt pocket before addressing Sidney. "Talk to me," she said.

So, Sidney told Wanda about her nightmares; visions for lack of a better word because what had happened was almost real, as if she were there in person. There was a recurring theme: some old church or gothic building surrounded by graves. Someone was waiting; and then that person, a man, was hit on the head and dragged off by two others. They looked like police, but their uniforms were green, not blue. He was moaning and crying out, but she couldn't remember what he was saying. The persons dragging this man seemed to be in a hurry. It was dark, and she couldn't see where they were going. Then she woke up.

Wanda leaned forward. "Can you remember what this man looked like?" she asked.

Sidney thought for a moment or two, hating to relive the nightmare again. "I'm not certain," she said.

"Try again, dear, and give me your hands for a moment, please," she said. Once Wanda had covered Sidney's hands with hers, she asked Sidney to look again and see if she could describe the man who had been dragged away. Quite suddenly the room seemed to spin around them, slowly at first, then faster and faster. Sidney began to feel as if she might throw up. Then the things around her vanished from view, and the nightmare began again.

Sidney was there, standing by the man. They were in a graveyard with a tall brick church in the background. It had stained-glass windows, but they were all dark. It was nighttime, windy and bitter cold. The man was frightened by something. Sidney could hear a siren in the distance. The man sat down on one of the graves. He was drinking out of a bottle. He wore a fuzzy cap that looked like a hat you'd wear to go skiing in. Suddenly there was a loud THWACK, and the man fell; large muscular arms grabbed him from behind Sidney tried to run, but her feet wouldn't move. She was terrified that the arms would come for her too. The man had dropped a bouquet of flowers. They were roses, but it was too dark to see the color. Using all her strength, she finally began running away, but her feet were heavy and her progress slow. She tried to scream for help, but nothing came out of her mouth. She heard one last thing, though, as the man was dragged off. "Do not speak to anyone", he said. And then she woke up.

Sidney could hear someone talking to her, but it seemed far away, and the words being said were vague. The dream had passed, but now she was in some kind of space between the dream and reality. Oppressed by the weight of the things that she had seen, she opened her eyes. The room was still whirling about her.

"She's coming back," she heard somebody say. It was Wanda's voice, but instead of being right next to her, it sounded very far off. She was paying all of her attention now to the voice: it was asking her to return.

The first thing she saw was Wanda sitting right where she had been, hands clasped in her lap. There were more lines of age in her face, or perhaps the light in the room had changed.

The sun was distinctly lower in the sky than when they had begun their session, and the sunrays had taken on an orange glow. Still, Sidney had the odd feeling that her dream had drained some of Wanda's vitality, but she could not imagine how such a thing could be.

Wanda was the first to break the silence. She coughed and shifted painfully in her chair and looked directly into Sidney's eyes. Her expression was one of tenderness and sadness. She was still speaking, and as Sidney's thoughts came into focus, the words came through to her, "...and give her grace, strength, and courage on this journey. Surround her with your angels; defend and protect her from all evil. Give her light in the time of darkness. We give thanks. Amen."

"I think you will be back with us soon," Wanda said. "There is no doubt in my mind that you have been given the gift of prophecy. I must warn you that the time is coming when you may be called upon to assist in defending against the Evil One, who we think has been able to make his way into the world by entering into the physical body of a man. This man is the perfect embodiment of all the aspirations of the Prince of Darkness and as such is the ideal 'vehicle.' There are signs, many signs, of the approach of the End Days."

Sidney still felt a bit shaky and dizzy, but now she experienced a rising sense of panic. "Great," she thought. "I've wandered into some weird, end-of-the-world cult. These people could be dangerous." It was not that she lacked a belief in good versus evil. Like the majority of people with graduate degrees, she was quite convinced that evil was afoot in the world in the form of climate-change deniers, white supremacists, neo-Nazis, immigration restrictionists, the NRA, the Republican Party; the list was endless. The moral universe of her education was as starkly binary as that of her Puritan ancestors, if not more so, and no more forgiving of sinners. It was just that any kind of religious talk gave her the creeps.

"I don't go in for that kind of stuff," she said. As she rose, she resisted the urge to jump up and run out screaming. "But I appreciate chatting, and I hope you have a nice rest of your day." She edged toward the door. "And thank you for your time," she added pertly.

"Of course, dear, but I do hope you will not underestimate your ability to see into the heart of things. Such a gift, and it is a gift, comes from God, and with it comes a responsibility," Wanda said.

Sidney vacillated for a moment between asking what that responsibility might be and leaving as expeditiously as possible. She quickly settled on leaving. "Thanks again," she said with a little involuntary curtsy. The man in the kitchen nodded to her as she passed through the dining room. She noticed that he had been clasping his hands in front of him as if praying. Sidney let herself out. She was thinking how good it would be to go home. For the first time in months, she was actually glad to live in a city, sirens and all.

Wanda grimaced as she eased herself out of her seat. She walked into the central hallway and stood at the foot of the stairs. Reaching into a pocket, she produced an ornate brass whistle and blew one piercing note. In answer, a small group began to assemble, seating themselves around the farm table. Wanda stood at one end. She waited for everyone to settle down and took a long, slow breath.

"It is as we feared," she announced grimly. "I know what happened to Joe."

$\mathscr{C}$hapter 6

Sidney and Dylan woke up early. It was Saturday, but they had forgotten to turn off the alarm on the clock-radio; and they awoke to the voice of an announcer predicting a warm, sunny day. The window in their bedroom had been opened a crack the night before, and they could hear birds chirping in the holly trees outside. Gray dawn light filtered through the window. Sidney basked in the pleasure of not having to jump out of bed and prepare for work. Dylan reflected irritably that his wife had left the alarm set. The clock was on her side of the bed, after all. He was about to turn over and remind her that it was her fault they had been awakened prematurely, when Sidney snuggled up behind him, put a languid arm around his waist, and purred in his ear, "Mmmm."

They spent the next hour in bed and rose in a good humor. Over coffee and toast, Dylan chattered about his job and where his new contacts might lead him. In fact, he had talked of little else over the last couple of days. Each time he retold his chance encounter and dinner with the two gentlemen from GOOD, he remembered some additional witticism of the brilliant historian Armand Black or some clever response that he himself had made. Dylan was not a systematic thinker. He was incapable of giving an accurate and circumstantial report of anything in a way that began at the beginning, continued to the end, and then stopped. Rather, he remembered selective snippets of conversation as related topics popped into his mind. But as much as he liked Dr. Black's quips and anecdotes, the subject that interested him the most was the tantalizing possibility of a job at this mysterious and apparently well-funded organization, GOOD. Black had hinted that he thought Dylan was eminently qualified to help write articles about cutting-edge technology and social programs. Of course, as an independent news writer, he had not allowed flattery or the lure of a possible job offer to influence his reporting on the new partnership between GOOD and the University. Fortunately, there was nothing negative to be said about it. A badly situated old church and graveyard with structural problems were to be whisked away to a more suitable location, and a magnificent modern tower would rise in their place. There, the best minds would design a new, rational world order, based on equality and diversity. Peace and justice would prevail. Mr. Wheedler had spoken at some length about the insanity of America trying to make the rest of the world look like the U.S.A. "It is time," he had said, "to make the U.S.A. look like the rest of the world." What right-thinking person could object to that?

This was the first time in months that Dylan had experienced excitement about anything. Sidney was thrilled to think this opportunity might be a step up for him; a chance to show what he was capable of: great writing and doing something more interesting and important than just reporting the news. Maybe now he would make enough money to realize their dream of moving to the country. She had decided earlier not to mention her own failure at the community college that week. There was still a lot to sort out. Had the students filed a complaint? Would the college punish her? Better not to think or speak of her uncertainty. She was happy to listen to her husband for once.

As he ran out of things to say, Dylan's exuberance led him to think about some way to celebrate his good fortune. An idea flashed into his mind. They could have an early lunch at a little café he had seen on 36th street, Café Hon. Perhaps they could grab a burger and then take a walk over to see the Baltimore Museum of Art. The café wasn't very far from their apartment, just a short jaunt down Roland Avenue, and the BMA was not much farther at all. "Let's explore today!"

he announced, as he hurried into the living room and rifled through the drawers of the desk.

"Aha!" He held up a glossy four-color brochure about Baltimore's sites of interest. He smiled. All of a sudden, it looked as if they were still a loving couple and not the strangers he feared they had become of late.

Sidney, not realizing that he was planning anything as interesting as a date, came out of the kitchen to see where he had gone. She looked perplexed and rumpled, trying to pull her terrycloth robe together.

"What are you doing?" she asked him.

"We're going out," Dylan said, "so let's get dressed before this beautiful day escapes us!"

"Where are we going?" Sidney asked. "What should I wear?"

Dylan was starting to feel pleased with himself that beautiful spring morning, and with his genius at figuring out that what they needed was to spend more time together. "We are going on a date," he said. "First, we'll get a little lunch, and then we can walk over to the art museum. It's not far either, just on the south side of the Johns Hopkins undergraduate campus."

Sidney beamed. She liked this new Dylan. Instead of questioning him, as she would normally have done, she simply said "Okay."

After several minutes of Sidney's primping in front of the bathroom mirror and Dylan's crawling under the bed to retrieve his sneakers, they were finally ready to be on their way. He opened the apartment door for her. They descended the stairs, first Sidney then Dylan, laughing at the novelty of leaving the house together. At the front door, she turned to smile back at Dylan but was surprised to see out of the corner of her eye that Mrs. Fitzgerald had also come out into the hall at the same time.

"I heard you laughing," Mrs. Fitzgerald said, "but I see that you are getting ready to go out, so maybe this isn't a good time to visit."

Dylan found his voice first. "What is it?" he asked.

Mrs. Fitzgerald shook her head. "Nothing really," she replied. "I had a notion that it might be nice if you two could join Evan and me for a light supper tonight?"

An uncomfortable silence followed. The one thing that Sidney and Dylan agreed upon was that privacy was essential to them, especially because they lived in such close proximity to their landlords. "We don't want to impose," Sidney said.

"Oh my, it wouldn't be an imposition, dear," Mrs. Fitzgerald said.

Sidney looked at Dylan, then back at Mrs. Fitzgerald. "That will be nice," she said, a little coolly.

"Wonderful. Is five o'clock too early to come down? Well, it's settled, then. See you at five. Enjoy your walk!"

Café Hon is just the place to stop and take in a bit of Baltimore oddness. There is a certain type of Baltimore matron, whose heyday was the era of the beehive hairdo, who addressed everyone as "hon." This *rara avis* is by no means extinct even now, and the center of her nesting range is the 19th-century industrial village of Hampden. Hence the name and location of the restaurant to which Sidney and Dylan strolled on this fine Saturday morning. Situated on the corner of Roland Avenue and 36th Street, the café sports a large pink flamingo above the door and a life-sized, full-color statue of Elvis Presley in the front of the dining room. The food is home-style American, in the best tradition of the diners of the 1950's. The cheerfulness of the place, and the sense of stepping back in time, gave a boost to the couple's already buoyant mood.

From the café, they wandered eastward along 36th Street, known to locals as "The Avenue," peering into the windows of antique shops. Then they strolled down Beech Avenue, skirting the edge of Wyman Park, and continuing past the lower parking lots of Johns Hopkins University. They paused on the edge of the campus to consult their tourist brochure.

"Look," said Dylan. "Here's another park across from the museum. There's supposed to be a statue."

They ran across Art Museum Drive to the place indicated in the pamphlet, but there was no statue to be seen, only an empty pediment in the center of a square. "Huh," said Dylan, "That was supposed to be a big statue of Generals Lee and Jackson. Oh, well, on to the museum."

There was enough in the museum to occupy the rest of the day. A special exhibit, by someone who appeared to be working under an alias, invited the visitor "to explore the dynamic of personal liberation" by looking at such creations as a set of nylon pantyhose stuffed with sand; a hanging cluster of deflated balloons which, according to the label, had once contained helium; three headless manikins in red-stained tuxedos, holding top hats; and a stuffed cat with its head stuck in a goldfish bowl. Outside, a sculpture garden featured a large spiky red thing, an assortment of geometric stones like the waste from a marble mill, and other dated banalities. Musing on the limited shelf life of avant-garde material, they went into the older part of the building and found a surprising sense of serenity in the timeless art of past centuries. It was as if the museum had been set up to produce this effect, or perhaps to prevent, by a sufficient separation, a cataclysmic reaction between art and anti-art, like the mutual annihilation of matter and anti-matter. Neither of the young people had been accustomed to move in circles where it was necessary to pretend to be impressed by objects that did not appeal to them.

On the other hand, they had absorbed enough cultural diffidence to refrain from poking fun at anything, no matter how ridiculous. Mercifully, the same attitude spared them the vexation of being angered or insulted by the imposture of bogus art. As a result, they passed a very pleasant and edifying afternoon, returning home with just enough time to shower and dress for dinner.

———————————

Dr. Fitzgerald met them at the door of the first-floor apartment and ushered them into the living room, where the dogs went through their barking ritual until everyone was seated. There was a fire burning brightly in the hearth, and the doctor asked what everyone would like to drink. Soon, all were settled in, Sidney with a glass of Chardonnay, Dylan ("I'll have whatever you're having") with a Manhattan on the rocks, the doctor with the same, and Mrs. Fitzgerald with a Margarita. As they nibbled cheese and crackers, they chatted about the art museum, the grand marble lions that stood in front of it, and other bits of statuary. The topic reminded Dylan of the missing statue in the park, and he commented that the guide book was in error.

"The information was correct when your guide was printed," said the doctor. "I'm surprised that you haven't heard about the removal! The city government took it away in the dark of night, as part of a purge of Confederate statues. Ostensibly, the mayor acted to remove an image that was offensive to blacks. No matter if its removal was offensive to whites. Whites don't count. We're the problem, you see. The truth is that most blacks were either unaware of the statue's presence or indifferent to it. This is just the latest assault in the ongoing cold civil war. Military defeat and humiliation are not enough for those people; they have to come back and desecrate the graves, topple the monuments. It's nothing to do with objective reality. Lee was a thoroughly decent and honorable man who opposed slavery. He was revered by all sorts of people, north and south, black and white. This and similar acts of vandalism are part of a program of anti-white genocide."

"Surely that's a bit strong!" protested Dylan.

"I define genocide as the elimination of a people and its culture. The same characters who are cheering on mass immigration from the third world, which is ultimately the replacement of the legacy population of the U.S. (I might add, to the detriment of the interests of our legacy black citizens as well), these same characters are pushing for the removal of public monuments to white men. The Confederate generals are just the beginning. Next, they'll come for Columbus, Jefferson, Washington, and on and on. Even Babe Ruth, for pity's sake! If you don't believe me, just wait and see." He took a sip of his Manhattan. "Oh, well, I guess by now you've written me off as a racist, which is to say, a person whose every utterance is to be ignored."

Dylan shifted uneasily in his chair. "Everyone's entitled to their own opinion," he offered.

The firelight reflected off Dr. Fitzgerald's white hair and ruddy, cheerful face. He was a gentleman, and he always did his best to conceal his distaste when someone said something particularly trite and ungrammatical. In his experience, most people who said what Dylan had just said meant exactly the opposite. He took another sip of his Manhattan. "I saw your article in the *Herald* about the plans for development of the Westminster Church site. What can you tell us about this organization G.O.O.D.? Is it true that Klaus Pyknos is behind it?"

"You must be referring to a conspiracy theory that's been circulating on some of the more extreme internet sites," said Dylan, with a chuckle. "Snopes has debunked it. I don't know anybody who takes that any more seriously than the rumor that Pyknos is funding rent-a-mobs like the anti-fascist counter-protesters in Charlottesville and Baltimore. Actually, from what I see, GOOD is all about making the world a better place."

Mrs. Fitzgerald had gone into the kitchen during this discussion, and now she returned to summon everyone into the dining room. A savory chicken and mushroom casserole, herbed rice, and asparagus kept them all occupied for a few minutes.

"So," began Dylan, turning toward his host, "from your accent, I take it you must be from the South."

Fitzgerald smiled. "Yes. I'm from Baltimore. You *do* know that the famous Mason-Dixon line marks the northern border of our state."

"But," objected Dylan, "Maryland stayed with the Union."

"Only because it was occupied by Federal troops, who terrorized the populace into submission. After dinner, I'll show you some things that passed down through my family from that tragic period."

Dessert was a dense, dark-chocolate mousse with whipped cream. Sidney helped Mrs. Fitzgerald with the dishes while the doctor poured after-dinner drinks and showed Dylan back to his study. The wall was hung with diplomas from Johns Hopkins, bearing the name Evan William Fitzgerald IV. There was an illegible framed document of great antiquity, bearing a thick seal of red wax. An 18th-century sabre and a brace of flintlock pistols hung over a glass case full of curious objects.

"Here," said the doctor, "is a small print of the painting *The Last Meeting of Jackson and Lee*, by Everett Julio, which was the basis for the equestrian monument that you were looking for on Art Museum Drive. I always find it very touching because it shows them in their last conversation before the death of Jackson at Chancellorsville. And it was at that same battle that Lee caught the strep infection that turned into rheumatic fever and ultimately killed him. Of course, Mark Twain, in his puerile, reductive way, wrote that the painting wouldn't be as poignant if it had a different title, like *Jackson asking Lee for a Match*. He was an early mocker and trivializer of a lost cause in which so many good people died. I happen to agree with him that the secessionists in the deep South were foolish, but in my opinion, Lincoln's resort to military coercion was plain evil.

"On that subject, in this drawer, I have a few letters from that time. This one from September 1864 was to inform my great-great grandfather of the death of his cousin, Billy McDonald, who owned a country estate called Guilford. There it is in a photograph from 1914, looking very forlorn, just before the Roland Park Company tore it down. You can see it was a huge Victorian mansion with a cupola on top. Cousin Billy lit a candle in the upper part of the house one night because he was looking for a newspaper or something; and the next morning, Yankee soldiers showed up and accused him of signaling to the enemy. They dragged him off to Fort McHenry and locked him up until he caught a lung infection. He died shortly after his release, at the age of 34. That kind of thing happened to a lot of very prominent Baltimoreans, though most of them were lucky enough not to die from their mistreatment.

"Well, enough of that. I'm sure I've bored you long enough, but this *is* information that you won't find everywhere. Shall we rejoin the ladies?"

The rest of the evening passed in light conversation about local attractions, the weather, and favorite movies. As Sidney and Dylan reentered their own apartment, they looked at each other and laughed. "Wow," said Dylan, "if I talked that way at work, I'd be out of a job! Really, white genocide!"

Sidney just shook her head. She had gone through any number of lectures, training sessions, vigils, and marches focusing on the wickedness of white people; but she had never thought that any of that antipathy could be directed at her. Having a clear conscience, she had always supposed that such educational events were necessary to enlighten others less pure than herself. The marches and prayer sessions had even given her a *frisson* of danger, as if she were marching with Martin Luther King. Even exercises in racial self-abasement, such as confessing her "white privilege" and apologizing for "unconscious bias" had felt comfortable, like the general confession in the Episcopal church she had attended as a child. Sometimes the ritual humiliation had been even more elevating, as if she were the innocent sacrificial Victim taking on the sins of the whole world. But a shadow had fallen across this sunny salvific vision, and it had begun in the classroom on Friday.

*C*hapter 7

Armand Black, Ph.D., was a meticulous man. His suits were lint-free and perfectly tailored. His shirts were crisp, and his Windsor-knotted neckties sported the crest of his Ivy-League alma mater. He drove a vintage BMW, which an early riser would have seen cruising the side streets of Roland Park, where he lived in a modest but architecturally correct Moorish-style cottage, circa 1928. He was a mere five minutes from where he had agreed to pick up the young reporter Dylan, but he had started an hour early so that he could commune with his fine automobile and some (mostly) decent architecture.

To suggest that Black was a snob would be to do him less than justice. He was above all else an aesthete. The son of a member of the diplomatic corps, he had spent the first fourteen years of his life in North Africa, where he had acquired a taste for the exotic and a fluency in French and Arabic that were to serve him well in his study of history. Regarding Arabs, he would not have disputed Houellebecq's description of "mendiants pleins de poux;"[3] but for their religion, especially in its highest and most austere manifestations, he had a genuine admiration. His attitude had nothing to do with Faith. Belief never entered into it. Violence, cruelty, even the most extravagant depravity, he could take in stride, at least in principle; but commonness, tawdriness, cheapness he despised.

His father had died suddenly when a Muslim "activist" blew himself up outside the American consulate, and young Armand had returned stateside with his mother, to live in her small hometown in the center of the country. Even today, forty-some years later, he winced at the memory of the painful adjustment: the bullying louts in his school, the tacky tract houses. His parents had always pronounced his given name in the French manner, and it did not occur to him until too late that his new classmates would mock him for it, holding their noses and mincing around with their hands in the air.

A different kind of boy might have attempted to get into the good graces of his schoolmates. Armand simply wrote them off as unworthy of his effort. A well-directed punch was all it took to shut up the chief bully and win himself some tentative acceptance, but he chose to keep aloof and to immerse himself in his studies. He had a retentive mind and a knack for discovering valuable artworks and antiques, enough to support himself through college and graduate school. He could sniff out forgeries and copies with an inerrancy that soon made him a valuable consultant to wealthy art collectors, including the wealthiest of all, Klaus Pyknos. That was more than twenty years ago, when he spotted a fake da Vinci and saved the old man a few million Euros. Pyknos was over seventy then but was still sailing, skiing, playing squash, and flying with his super-model mistresses to Como, Gstaad, Antibes…ah! Beautiful places where the vulgar herd could not follow. Since then, Armand had attached himself to Pyknos like a remora on a giant shark, and he had fed richly.

Black was still smiling at pleasant memories as he eased his car up to the curb in front of the young reporter's house. He was several minutes early. Precise punctuality was more to his taste, but this was a test. How would the boy respond? Would he be caught by surprise? No. The front door of the house opened, and Dylan loped easily down the steps, opened the passenger door, and offered a bright "Good morning!"

"Ready for a day in the country?" asked Black, turning on the windshield wipers. They drove for about forty minutes, as the spring shower gave way to a heavy rain. Neither made an attempt at conversation. It seemed as if they must be almost to Pennsylvania when they approached a massive gate that swung open at the touch of a keypad. A long, tree-lined drive led to a fieldstone farmhouse with a wide front porch. A portico extended out beyond the porch, so that they were able to stay dry. The front door opened before them as if by magic; but as they entered, Dylan saw that a grim-faced, bald Asian man in a black suit was holding the door handle and eyeing him suspiciously. There was no time to form an impression of the interior of the house, for Black walked briskly down the center hall and into an entirely different sort of building.

They strode down a long, gray corridor, lit by fluorescent tubes and devoid of any decoration. At one point, they stopped at a security door, which opened only after Black put his right eye to a metal box on the wall. Another passage of even greater length brought them to a double door of stainless steel, which opened to reveal a conference room with a table and thirty chairs. The decor was what Dylan thought of as "Euro Techno," all metal and molded plastic, with a gray laminate tabletop. A large, rain-spattered picture window looked out on a perfectly round pond and a wide horse pasture with white-painted fences.

"Good morning, Mr. Greene," said a voice from the end of the room. Dylan started and looked around. Mr. Wheedler was sitting at one end of the conference table. The little gray man blended in so well as to be almost invisible. "Your article on the, uh, development project was just right." He smacked his lips as if enjoying the taste of it. "Yes, just right. Help yourself to some coffee. I think the light is dim enough without closing the blinds."

He touched a remote control, and a huge screen at the end of the room lit up with the GOOD logo: a globe with a happy face. A series of slides followed, with mission statements, complex organizational charts, and photos of suffering African refugees, whose resettlement in the United States and Europe appeared to be the organization's main international focus at present. Mr. Wheedler's halting, tentative speech was not easy to listen to, and today it appeared that he had caught a cold, as he had to stop and blow his nose every few words. Dylan's attention began to drift as the slides changed faster and faster.

"Oh, yes," Wheedler was saying, as he backed up to the third slide before last, "the domestic agenda in the U.S. Here we are. Of course, there are the usual, uh, uncontroversial ongoing efforts to stop gun violence, close the racial achievement gap, etcetera, all of which dovetail nicely with our new international law institute, which will be such a force for change that we can expect to see outdated stuff like the U.S. Constitution go completely by the, uh, wayside, not that anyone who matters takes it seriously anyway. The future is global!"

Blowing his nose again, he carefully added another wadded paper napkin to the growing pile on the table. "Now we come to our public-private partnership efforts for order and safety." The slide showed smiling GOOD police men and women in green uniforms. Every breed of homo sapiens appeared to be represented in the group photo. "I hope your paper will endorse our efforts to help Baltimore City with its, shall we say, staffing difficulties in the police department. But we can come back to that." He flashed through a half-dozen slides, then stopped on one that showed a printed circuit, magnified to fill the screen. "Now, look at this! Our scientists are ready right now to roll out our, uh, Easy Chip initiative. Imagine having an implanted chip that lets you breeze through airport security or buy food at the supermarket even if you forgot your wallet. Or just suppose, what if the *police* catch you driving without your wallet? Ooh, trouble, right? But with an Easy Chip, the officer can instantly confirm your identity and the status of your driver's license. No fuss, no hassle!"

"Won't people think that's kind of an invasion of their privacy?" asked Dylan.

"Oh, I don't think so. It will be, um, encoded and, um, password-protected. And suppose something, uh, untoward happened to you, and the authorities needed to make the necessary calls; all the relevant information would be instantly available, even if you were, uh, unable to communicate. I've taken the liberty to enter what would appear on your personal profile on Easy Chip Version 1.0. As you see on this slide, there is a wealth of information here. Your Social Security and bank account numbers are X-ed out of course for purposes of demonstration, but there's your wife Sidney and her birth date and account numbers, even your landlord's name, see: Evan William Fitzgerald, IV, M.D., internal medicine specialist, and..."

Armand Black, who had been sitting with his eyes more than half closed, jumped as if he had been poked with a cattle prod. Immediately regaining his composure, he smoothed his hair and said, "Sorry. I must have started to doze off. Tell me about your landlord, Dylan. You don't see too many Fourths running around."

"Him? Oh, just an old guy approaching retirement. Old-fashioned ideas. Comes from an old Baltimore family, with lots of old stuff, you know, pictures, letters, deeds, books, curios."

Black chuckled amiably. "Of course. I know the type." Then he looked at his watch and said, "Oops, I'm late for a meeting upstairs. Sorry. Be back shortly!" As the door closed behind him, Messrs. Wheedler and Greene stared at each other in puzzlement.

Once out of the conference room, Armand Black opened an unmarked door and rushed up a spiral staircase, taking the steps two at a time. When he burst through the door at the top, a white-haired man with a tidy goatee stood up and looked at him reproachfully.

"I'm sorry, sir. Did you ring for an appointment?" he asked stiffly.

"Chambers, you know perfectly well I didn't ring. But I have to speak to the Chair! It's urgent! Here," and he scribbled a note. "Here, give him this!"

A voice over an intercom rasped, "Let him in, you old twit!"

"The Chair will see you now," announced Chambers. He shuffled toward an ornately carved wooden door and opened it.

Dr. Black pulled down the front corners of his vest and straightened his lapels. A cloud of incense assailed his nostrils as he entered the next room. There, behind an iron-bound Hinoki-wood desk, sat a very short, thick-set man with jet-black hair. His eyes had an unnerving intensity, and his compact frame suggested dangerous reserves of strength. Yet he sat in a motorized wheelchair.

"I think I've located the missing cipher!" exclaimed Black without preamble.

"Really. And you think it will make a difference? We already know that what we want is in Poe's grave," replied the Chair.

"Yes, but there was a piece missing. The document I, shall we say, 'liberated' from the archives in Richmond is only the rough draft. I think I know where to look for the actual letter and the enclosed coded message! This is essential due diligence!"

Klaus Pyknos smiled. He liked enthusiasm in his underlings, within limits. And he had profited before, and even avoided substantial losses, through Armand's attention to detail. "Very well," he said. "Get it." He cleaned his fingernails with the tip of a long, finely-wrought Italian dagger. "By the way, you outdid yourself when you found this beauty. The poignards of the quattrocento were truly unsurpassed, eh?"

Armand Black bowed slightly in acknowledgement of the compliment. He had, in fact, curated all the furnishings of the office when the Chair's fancy had shifted to a Japanese theme. The dagger alone had survived the make-over. Now, rice-paper wall hangings, carved screens, vases with courtly figures, jade statuettes, a complete suit of Samurai armor, several edged weapons, tatami mats, and a tea set completed the tableau. The armor, though, was the most striking presence in the room. Standing opposite the desk, it looked like a sinister black knight, or a horned demon, with a face mask sprouting fake whiskers. The sight of it gave Chambers the creeps.

"Consider it done," said Black.

When his manservant (historian, antiquarian, consultant, whatever) had left the room, Pyknos spun his wheelchair around and looked out the window. He had lived a full life. Now, paradoxically, at the height of his power, he stood to lose it all. He closed his eyes. She was still a bittersweet memory, the pretty little *puta*! It happened on a pleasure trip with a former President of the United States. The setting was a vast ranch in Mexico, just below the border. Some prime *señoritas* had been brought in from nearby Acuna. At the height of his amorous exertions, something had gone wrong. The cocaine, he was sure, had had nothing to do with what his doctors called a "vascular accident" (charming euphemism). Now he was an invalid, scarcely strong enough to stand. And every day he felt the cold hand of death's angel upon his shoulder.

Not that he had failed to foresee his own demise or to plan for it! On the contrary, a full decade earlier, he had engaged the best computer technicians to create a Mind, oh yes, a Master Mind that could carry on after his own fleshly brain was reduced to ash and scattered in his favorite parts of the Mediterranean. It had a neural network that learned by pattern recognition, just like a human brain. For years, he had been training it to think as he thought, speak as he spoke. As soon as he died, this Mind was set to activate upon the flat-lining of his cardiac monitor, and it would run his empire in his stead. But then, one day, the Mind beat him at chess; and it occurred to him that this Mind was not Pyknos. It would never be Pyknos. This Mind would continue to organize itself without him, and it would quickly become another mind entirely. Certainly not his! And so, he had given orders to switch it off. The red LED's had blinked once and gone dark, and the Mind that was not really his mind had gone to sleep in the lowest basement of the building.

He was happy with his own mind just the way it was. Not many men could manipulate the world as he had learned to do. Starting with a substantial fortune (his father was a shipping magnate), he had learned how to crash the economies of small countries for his own profit. It was pitifully easy. You persuaded them to go into debt for some extravagant project (an airport, a highway system, electrification), and when they couldn't repay, your bank owned the country. Or you crashed the currency through derivatives. Ka-ching! Or you stirred up a revolution, or a strike, or a civil war. Setting disparate ethnic groups against each other required so little effort and paid such huge dividends. Ah, diversity is strength, for those who manage it! After a while, figuring out how to profit from these situations was child's play. But the United States—that was proving a harder nut to crack. All he needed was time, but time was running out.

He turned back to his desk and picked up the letter that Armand had stolen for him. It was in a shiny acetate sheath that reflected the rain-specked window. He tilted the paper so that he could read it.

To Dr. Evan Fitzgerald, 2nd February, 1873
My Dear Sir,

I am now in receipt of yours of the 25th ult., it having been forwarded to me from the offices of the Evening Post. The account I am about to give is of a confidential nature, and not merely because it tarnishes my own reputation for veracity. But you will see. I entrust to you this confidential missive, this vera confessio, out of the love I bear you as an old friend.

Imprimis, I beseech you to forgive me for any seeming imputation of laxness or impropriety on the part of your father. I regret that I never had the honor of his acquaintance, and I most certainly did not know that he served as an election Judge in Baltimore at the time of Poe's death.

So many years and so many sorrows have flowed over us since that fateful October of

1849. My health has been delicate for some time, and well I know that my own days are numbered, and that my weary soul must return anon to the bosom of Him "from whom no secrets are hid." In laying upon you the burden of this confidence, I flatter myself that I may hope to be acquitted in your estimation of the charge of slandering your sire.

Edgar Poe was, as all have acknowledged, a tragic genius, a fragile giant. He had a sharp pen, and he made many enemies. Yet none of his literary "hatchet jobs" earned him as much hatred as his betrothal to his childhood sweetheart Elmira, whose family had spurned him away years before. As a rich widow in 1849, Elmira was free to marry whom she chose. But alas, her three brothers, George, James, and Alexander Royster by name, regarded Poe as a fortune hunter and vowed to kill him or at least render him hors de combat. To their bitter antipathy and their bloody plot, Poe was oblivious. His fears lay in another direction entirely, for he had discovered the secret of everlasting life, a discovery to which he incautiously alluded in his last

*great work, aptly entitled "Eureka." Unscru-
pulous men in the employ of one of the great
northern industrial magnates were following
close upon his trail wherever he went, hoping
to waylay him and seize certain materials
which he possessed, encompassing both the
secret and the means of attaining immortality.*

*Traveling north from Baltimore toward
Philadelphia by train, Poe became aware of
the presence of these hired ruffians in a seat
behind him. Ever resourceful, he gave them
the slip and, through the help of an acquaintance, lay low for a few days before returning
to Baltimore incognito. He suffered his well-
known mustache to be shorn off and arrayed
himself in cast-off clothes of the shabbiest description imaginable.*

*But alas! The Royster brothers found him
out, not through any cleverness of their own
(a quality, be it said, that none had ever remarked in them) but by sheer chance. They
quite literally ran into him on the station platform. Suspecting nothing and desirous of
maintaining a friendly intercourse with his
new in-laws, the poet reluctantly succumbed*

to their entreaties to break his recent pledge of abstinence from ardent spirits and accompanied them to a saloon in the eastern part of the city. The delicate workings of Poe's brain were soon unstrung by cheap whisky. When they were satisfied that he was helplessly stupefied by drink, the Royster brothers beat him insensible and left him for dead.

These facts I know from sources whose names I may not reveal while they live. I also know from the same unimpeachable individuals that the materials which the other villains had sought to purloin had been secreted in a compartment of Edgar's traveling trunk. This trunk he had taken with him from Richmond. After his death, a Baltimore physician (one Dr. Moran) discovered it in storage and turned it over to Edgar's cousin Neilson Poe, who is sworn to inter its secret contents with his kinsman's mortal remains as soon as a suitable stone marker may be carved.[4] Neilson, tho' not exceedingly fond of his cousin, is nonetheless sensible of his fame, and, as I believe, craves the vicarious honor thereby conferred upon the Poe family. So far from being

*interested in the promise of everlasting life, he
has told me personally that he "would sooner
die and go to h——- than drag a deathless body
through this vale of tears 'forever more.'"*

*I pray you to understand that when, some
time after the late war (a tragedy of such pro-
portions as to divert all my energies and re-
duce all else to insignificance), I concocted
the story of Poe being "cooped" by ruffians
during the election and compelled to cast
fraudulent votes, I desired only to cover the
trail, not only of affairs discreditable to the
family of his beloved Elmira, but perhaps also,
though Heaven only knows, of a powerful secret best kept buried.*

*I remain, with the most abject apologies
for any distress I may have caused you,*

Yrs. Truly,
Jno. R. Thompson[5]

*P.S. The enclosed scrap of paper was handed
to me by E. A. Poe himself just before his fateful departure from Richmond. It was rolled up
in the ms. of his poem "Annabel Lee." Ob-*

viously, it is some kind of cipher, but its solution has eluded me. Perhaps you will be able to make sense of it.

He laid the letter back on his desk. What were the odds that Poe was really onto something? Worth the gamble, surely. He would be a poor businessman if he couldn't make the gamble worth his while: dig up the "materials" in question while strengthening his grasp on the U.S. of A. and moving his chess pieces into alignment in the Culture War. Everything was going according to plan: the proximity of his headquarters to the Capital made it easy to keep a close rein on his "Menagerie" as he called them, the elephants and jackasses harnessed to his triumphal chariot. Bipartisanship! Such a lovely concept. Both parties, with only a few troublesome exceptions, fully endorsed his program. Whoever came up with the phrase, "Invade the world; invite the world" had summed it up nicely. Stir things up abroad. Keep the "refugees" coming. Rub the racist rubes' noses in diversity. Set the bastards against each other. Break the dollar to pay for it all. Guess who's waiting to pick up the winnings!

Pyknos removed his wig and rubbed the blotchy dome of his head. Such a brain in there! He scratched a scab, and it bled a little. (Note to self: don't scratch the scabs.) His eyes settled on the Samurai armor. The mouth of the mask had a cruel twist that he found compelling. "It speaks to me," he would tell Chambers. It was his private joke, between him and the Samurai. Because it *did* speak to him, and it showed him things he needed to see. As he gazed into the pitiless eyes of the mask, his own eyes kindled with a livid flame, and his mouth drifted open.

$\mathcal{C}$hapter 8

Down in the board room, Mr. Wheedler decided not to wait
for his impetuous colleague to return. He had a desk full of
legal documents requiring the application of more obscure
language, and he was eager to get back to them. He stood up
and wiped his glasses. "Come along, young man," he said.
"We need to get you a security clearance."

Dylan followed him out into the hall. To their right were the
metal doors of an elevator. Once inside, he saw that there were
six levels. They were on the fifth. Wheedler pressed the button
labelled 1. When they reached the bottom, Dylan reckoned that
they must be three stories underground. The hall that they entered was painted a darker shade of gray, almost charcoal, and
the walls were of concrete block. A barred door blocked their
way. It was of heavy steel like the door of a jail cell and painted

a dismal shade of green. Wheedler pressed an intercom button and announced himself. "Assistant Counsel here, with Mr. Greene." He looked up into the security camera. A buzzing noise arose from the door lock. With an effort, Wheedler pushed the massive grate inward and gestured for Dylan to go through.

The long hallway was devoid of decoration. Nothing interrupted the gray walls but a few flat black doors, some of which stood open. The jail door clanged shut. Dylan turned around to see his guide standing *outside* the bars. "Trapped like a rat!" were the words that arose in his mind.

"It's the third door on the left," said Wheedler, pointing down the hall. "Captain Bollard is our head of security. She will, um, process you. I'll send Dr. Black along when he returns." Sneezing and coughing, he turned toward the waiting elevator, stepped into it, and disappeared.

The third door was part-way open. It led into an office with white walls and gray metal file cabinets. On one wall was a bank of video monitors evidently showing various parts of the building and grounds. In the center of the room was a heavy black desk, and behind the desk sat a person in a green police uniform. The face was square-jawed but not quite masculine, and the dark brown hair was cropped close, so that the hair on top stood up like bristles on a brush. The visible portion of the upper body was large and muscular, with a very pronounced bust that stretched the uniform and caused it to gap open half an inch in the middle, revealing a glimpse of a black undergarment. Dylan concluded that it was a woman, though he was prepared to alter his assessment according to the individual's professed gender identity. A sign on the desk read, "Capt. Livvy Bollard."

The captain did not lift her eyes from the desk. She was reading from a paper in a file folder with the exaggerated attentiveness of a person concerned with appearing both busy and important. Dylan knocked gently on the open door and found that he might as well have rapped his knuckles on marble, so solid was the panel, and his knock was scarcely audible. There was no response from the captain, and he felt his face reddening as he worried that such a weak knock would mark him as a wimp. Was she toying with him?

Having allowed him just enough time to dwell on his doubts but not enough time to speak, Captain Bollard said, "All right. I know you're there." Only then did she deign to look up, and Dylan discovered that he had been less uncomfortable when she was looking down. Her gaze was contemptuous, cynical, and searching. In its focus, he perceived himself as a suspect, a cornered fugitive. "We have all the necessary information," she said, closing the file folder and handing it to him. "All you need to do is read it over and sign on page four to attest to its accuracy."

As Dylan perused the detailed summary of his personal information, he could feel her eyes upon him. She held out a pen. All was in order. He signed.

"There are just a few more formalities—photographs, fingerprints, blood and urine samples, you know, the usual," she said, rising from her chair and walking around the desk to stand between him and the door. She pushed the door, and it closed with a dull clank. "We have a few rules here that you need to know about. Actually, the whole manual of conduct is about 85 pages. You will sign an agreement to abide by those rules." As she spoke, she moved closer until he found himself backed against the desk. She was only about an inch taller than he was, but she seemed to tower over him. Now the front of her was pressed against him. He was conscious of a subtle cologne. She wore red lipstick which accentuated her sardonic half-smile. For a moment, he thought he felt a bulge in her pants that brushed against his own. He dismissed the thought with a shudder. She was still talking, saying something about enforcement and discipline; but trapped between her and the desk, he was having difficulty paying attention.

The phone rang on her desk. She let it ring three times before moving to pick it up. "Yes. That's right, professor, I have him. Oh, maybe an hour. I'll have my sergeant call you when we're done with him."

As she spoke, she stared steadily into Dylan's eyes, as a cat stares into the eyes of a bird. Putting down the receiver, she sat down again in her chair. "That was your friend Professor Black," she said with a note of disdain. "Do know what a professor is?"

Dylan shrugged.

"A professor is the guy who sits in the front parlor of the whorehouse and plays the piano but doesn't know what's going on upstairs." The corners of her mouth drew outward in a restricted smile, and she swayed very slightly from side to side, savoring the witticism. "Now, take this card and go all the way to the end of the hall. Sergeant Nyonga will handle you from here on." Pointedly opening another folder, she began to read its contents and made a motion with her left hand as if to sweep him away. He complied immediately.

The office at the end of the corridor had a small antechamber with two hard chairs. There were a few posters on the wall related to employment discrimination regulations and influenza vaccination requirements. A clear acrylic window looked through to a reception desk, but there was no receptionist to be seen. A sign taped to the window read, "Take a seat. The officer on duty will be with you shortly." Dylan obeyed.

There was no reading matter in the waiting room. A door to the right of the plastic pane evidently opened into the room behind, but it seemed inadvisable to try the knob. Intermittent muffled sounds came from somewhere behind the door. After ten minutes or so, Dylan stood up, bent his face down to the level of the semicircular aperture at the bottom of the window, and called, "Hello!" After a pause, he heard footsteps approaching. A jet-black woman in a green uniform appeared behind the window. Her hair was shaved very short, and she spoke with a lilting accent that seemed either Caribbean or native African.

"This office be closed on Sunday," she said. "You need somet'ing, you come back tomorrow."

"Oh," said Dylan. "I'm sorry. The head of security just sent me down here to go through, I guess, finger printing and all." He held up the card that Captain Bollard had given him. It had a magnetic strip on one side and his name hand-written in pencil on the other. The officer gestured for him to push it through the hole, then turned it over and over as if she had never seen one like it before.

She frowned. "HR be closed today too. Must be they computer off." She opened the door and instructed him to follow her.

In the back of the office was a folding table, and on it was an electronic contraption. The sergeant switched it on, then turned on a nearby computer. Next, she led Dylan to a chair on the other side of the computer and had him sit while she swung a camera into position. He waited while she logged onto the computer and opened a couple of programs. Then she asked for his name. After his name, she needed his birth date, address, and so on, until Dylan concluded that Sunday was not the best day to have shown up. Either that or the computers did not talk to each other, and he was sure that no such inefficiency could be possible in as forward-thinking an organization as GOOD.

The picture-taking was easy, but the finger-printing required several attempts, with exactly the right rolling motion of the fingertip on the electronic pad; and then it appeared that the last stage of transmission of the fingerprints "hung up," and the entire process had to be repeated. Two hours later, he held in his hand a very official-looking laminated ID badge with his photograph and an embedded chip. It identified him as "Associate Director, GOOD Institute," which seemed almost certainly wrong, but he decided that asking questions would only prolong the ordeal. To his relief, the Personnel Health Office was closed.

Sergeant Nyonga escorted him through the barred door. He saw no point in asking her what to do next, and so he took the elevator back to the fifth floor and reentered the boardroom. There, he found Armand Black, who had made some coffee and opened a package of peanut-butter-and-cheese crackers.

"Have a snack," Black suggested. "Now that you have a badge, it will be easier to show you around without tripping an alarm. This facility is the brain, or at least the central ganglion, of a worldwide superorganism." He downed the last swallow of coffee in his cup and went to pour himself some more.

"You mean the Global Outreach Organizing for Diversity?" asked Dylan.

"That and a great deal more than that. I like to think that GOOD, of which this is the headquarters, leads the rest of the world's progressive organizations, but it would probably be more accurate to say that we are the most important nerve center in a vast network. We constantly adapt. Sometimes we have to change the words we use. Sometimes we even have to 'pivot' for political purposes, but our game is a long game, and our focus is on the goal."

"Which is?"

"My boy, you wouldn't be here if you didn't already know the answer to that question. The United States and western Europe spent the last half a millennium exploiting the rest of the world and enriching themselves beyond any reasonable measure. Our goal is quite simply to rectify that situation, by (to coin a phrase) *any means possible.*" He slapped his hand on the table to emphasize the last three words. "The most effective strategy toward that goal is the transformation of western countries through importation of non-western peoples. It is a bold and beautiful initiative, the likes of which the world has never seen before. If you think about it, the kind of change that we are achieving used to be accomplished by armed invasion, where you kill the men and take the women as sex slaves. We have worked out how to do it all peacefully! How's that for progress? The invading army just walks in unopposed. All that's required is the administration of anesthesia."

Dylan raised his eyebrows. "What do you mean, anesthesia?"

"Oh, it's doctrinal, not pharmacologic," Black chuckled. "All the schools, all the mainline churches, what do they teach? That white people are guilty and need to atone for their sins against humanity. That they need to reach out for forgiveness to people of color. America's entire immigration policy since 1965 has been designed to bring in people from anywhere but Europe. In England, France, Holland, it's actually against the law to speak against the racial transformation of your country. We're at the point now where even in America, the yahoos can't whine about immigration without being called out for their racism. That's what I mean by anesthesia. It's far less painful to envision your grandchildren growing up as a despised racial minority in the country their ancestors built than it is to be branded a racist in the here-and-now. Of course, we've had to upgrade the insult to 'white supremacist' lately, but you get the idea.

"Let me give you a little tour. The place is pretty quiet on Sundays, but we do have critical personnel on duty 24-7."

Black led the way back to the elevator, and they descended to the third floor. As the door opened, they saw a hallway papered with gigantic satellite images of the earth. The photographs were enlarged to eight feet in diameter, so that they extended from floor to ceiling, and ran contiguously like beads in a giant's necklace. Each globe in the series was turned an eighth of a rotation to the east, in relation to the one before it. The display was interrupted only by the gray frames and knobs of the doors, for the wallpaper covered the flat surfaces of the doors as well.

One door stood open. Dr. Black said "Ahem" as he approached, then paused before stepping to the door. Within the office, a chair creaked, and there was a shuffling of feet. "Justin!" said Black cheerily, "I'd like you to meet Dylan Greene. I'm showing him around. Dylan, this is Justin Goldstein, our team-leader for news analysis."

Dylan took a step into the room and shook what proved to be a lean, limp hand. It was attached to an arm of equal thinness, which connected to a bespectacled personage in a white polo shirt with a GOOD logo on the left breast. Dylan imagined that if he did an internet search for "Geek" and selected "Images," this particular specimen would appear at the top of the display.

Justin looked up for a moment, saw Dylan's new ID badge, and turned back to his computer.

"Anything exciting?" asked Black.

"Oh, Twitter is still cheeping about whether Babe Ruth is offensive to blacks. It's a slow day, so I've been sending out a few tweets just to see if I can provoke some embarrassing reactions. But I think we've wrung this one dry."

Black laughed appreciatively. "I was just telling Dylan here about our long-range mission of societal transformation through peaceful invasion."

Justin winced. "I don't think I would put it quite that way," he said. "But I guess you could, among ourselves, that is. Your choice of words probably wouldn't play well out in fly-over country. We have to be disciplined about how we say things. The gates of Troy are open, so to speak, and the Trojans are letting in not just one, but a whole herd of wooden horses crammed with Greeks. It's almost comical. But keeping those gates open requires an effort. Our opponents are quick to publicize every crime committed by aliens. To counter them, we have to keep up a multi-pronged campaign against white identity. The campaign against the Confederate flag and the leaders of the Confederacy was a textbook case of what I'm talking about. Now between you and me, I don't really believe that there are many Klansmen running around, but it's important to create the perception that there are. So, we wait for some crazy guy like this fellow Roof in South Carolina who shoots up a black church. Fortunately, he had a picture taken of himself with a Confederate battle flag. He saved us the trouble of photo-shopping it. Then we set the outrage machine in motion, and bingo! People start taking down flags all over the place. Big box stores stop selling them. (It's fun to pressure *them*; they *always* give in.) Next, a few demonstrations and spray-paintings, and most of the Confederate monuments come down. And I don't mean just the generals. Hey, Baltimore even took down a monument to Confederate *women*! A bronze statue of women grieving over a dying man!

"Or let's say we find out that some right-wing bastard is going to give a speech. All it takes is a few complaints or threats of demonstrations to get him cancelled. Hotels are afraid of disturbances. Colleges don't want to deal with costs of security. If the speech is to be in a public place, then, oh, yeah, that's where we really shine. Charlottesville was managed perfectly. There was a planned demonstration, with a permit, against the removal of a statue of Robert E. Lee. I don't know whether the Antifascist and Black-Lives-Matter counter-protesters were paid for by us, but I think they were. Anyway, the police cooperated to create maximum conflict so that the pro-monument suckers had to clear out without even getting a chance to speak. That way, *we* got to define who they were and what they thought. And the fat girl getting run down and killed, that was a bonus. That was the excuse for the removal of even *more* white supremacist monuments. See, each incident, if you manage it right, creates a half-dozen more opportunities. It's like a nuclear chain-reaction. Or a really cool computer game!"

He turned to his computer screen and pointed at a list of news reports. "Here's what we got so far from the Babe Ruth riot. Our analyst in Alexandria posted this:

"1- The Republican governor's security detail rushed him away, which made him look weak, and the Mayor of Baltimore gave the opening speech, with some comments about the need to remedy the history of prejudice and under-representation of African-Americans in base-ball, as well as a repetition of her earlier calls for the Babe Ruth statue to be removed to a baseball museum, where it will not "offend the conscience and inspire violent acts against people of color." Some of the crowd booed her, leading to criticism of white supremacist baseball fans by commentators on CNN, NBC, and NPR.

"2- Pro-statue protesters were effectively linked to Nazism. The lone Nazi flag-bearer has not been identified, but pictures of him have appeared in every televised news report. Glen Beck devoted part of his radio show the next morning to denouncing Nazis, saying that they are "not conservatives but leftists" and reminding his audience that Nazi is short for National Socialist. He ridiculed the Mayor for attacking Babe Ruth. No major outlet interviewed the man who was going to address the rally.

"3- Enough pro-statue protesters were arrested and/or injured to send a message to opponents of the removal of white supremacist statues in the future.

"And the report goes on with a list of specific commentary, but you get the gist of it. The crazy thing is that the Babe Ruth business wasn't even our idea. I mean, our plans did not include targeting that particular statue, but we saw what was happening, mobilized our assets, raised the level of conflict, seized control of the narrative, and advanced our cause. That's organizing! That's what you are going to love about being here!"

"Well," interrupted Black, "We don't know yet whether Dylan is actually going to *be* here. That question is still open.

And I believe I am not speaking out of turn if I say that Dylan's skills lie primarily in shaping the narrative *after* the fact. He's a writer for the *Baltimore Herald*."

Justin's eyes grew wide. The effect was magnified by his glasses. "Geez, I thought…He has an ID badge!"

"Oh, don't worry," laughed Black, placing a hand on Dylan's shoulder. "He's completely with us."

Dylan felt two sets of eyes observing his response. He felt like a hotdog lover touring the hotdog factory. Although he felt reasonably sure that he still liked the product, he was a little unsettled. "A thousand percent!" he said confidently. He remembered how disappointed he had been to find the Lee and Jackson statue gone. He liked historic sculptures. It could just as well have been Caesar or Napoleon. He didn't have to back their causes to enjoy their statues. His mind went back to a list he had seen of other notable statues in the tourist pamphlet.

"So," he asked, "What's the plan for the other statues?"

Justin gave him a blank look.

"You know," continued Dylan, "the other statues in Baltimore. There's the Edgar Allan Poe statue on the University of Baltimore campus. I'm pretty sure Poe used the n-word in at least a couple of his stories, and the sculptor was a decorated Confederate veteran. The big monument to Watson[6] on North Avenue must be offensive to Mexicans…"

"Okay, right," said Justin, "I see where you're going. Yeah, there's not a single statue of a white man that shouldn't come down. But it all takes time. You know the saying, 'Rome wasn't built in a day.' Well, it didn't fall in a day either. We push too hard and too fast, and there can be a reaction. We have to get more Hispanics in Baltimore before we go after the Mexican War statues. We don't need a *lot* more, but it's a process. They're busy doing landscaping and construction, and they don't know who the fuck Watson was. We could work through Casa de Maryland and La Raza and have them steamed up in a couple of weeks, but remember we have to bring in *more* of them to have an impact.

"Poe is pretty much off limits for now, on account of the Baltimore Ravens football team. What do you think, one in a thousand Ravens fans has actually read anything by Poe, even if they know he wrote 'The Raven'? And the black racial angle? Now, don't get me wrong, but you can't play chess if you think a pawn is a knight; you know what I mean? Blacks don't read. I mean, that's how you have to figure it if you want to advance the cause.

"When I was, like, twelve years old, I thought John Brown was the coolest dude in American history. First, he wiped out all those crackers in Kansas, and then he actually captured the U.S. arsenal at Harpers Ferry. I mean, he was kicking ass. But he made one huge mistake, and it got him killed. He expected the blacks to rally to him and actually arm themselves with all the weapons he had just scored. They never showed up! They never *will* show up when you need them! At least that has to be the way you look at it. In a video game, every tool or weapon that you pick up has a defined range of functions and limitations, and frankly in that kind of analysis, the blacks are kind of at the level of a rock. Not a heat-seeking missile. A rock. You just have to know how to use all your tools."

Dylan nodded slowly, as if absorbing this lesson in practical activism. He was about to say how much he resented the casual racism of the remark, but he sensed that such an objection would make him look like a dummy. He began to understand that he was in the presence of a progressive mastermind. This dweeby guy, this video gamer, was actually a ruthless revolutionary, in a sedentary, 21st-century way.

"I see," said Dylan. "You're like a general assessing the relative strengths and weaknesses of different parts of your army."

"Yeah, that's basically it. I like that analogy. And, as it implies, the object is to win the war."

"See, African-Americans aren't the future anyway," Justin went on. "They are still useful as a permanent seething reservoir of anti-white resentment. They aren't smart enough to ever do any better than they're doing now, relative to everybody else. You might think after sixty years of affirmative action and hundreds of billions spent on education, they'd realize they were running out of excuses. But hey, along comes 'white privilege' and 'structural racism,' and what do you know, it's still whitey's fault that Deshawn isn't a rocket scientist. Obviously, if all races are equal in IQ and behavioral and personality traits, then the only possible explanation for different outcomes is that those white devils are cheating. So, we can count on African-Americans to extract concessions out of the power structure from time to time by alternating between violence and victimhood, but they're being phased out."

"What do you mean, phased out?"

"Well, they'll be useful for another fifteen, twenty years, tops. We'll still be able to use them as a wedge to drive into a lot of cracks."

Dylan was beginning to feel that he really didn't like this guy. "I thought you said they were rocks. Now they're wedges," he growled.

"Ha, that's good. Right, you're a writer. Can't mix the metaphors. But a wedge is just a sharp rock. Anyway, they're going to be overwhelmed by all the new immigrants, who, trust me, don't have any sentimental attachment to Old Black Joe. Latin-Americans and African Muslims are going to outbreed what we could call the native blacks, who are barely reproducing at replacement rate. So, the descendants of both the slaves *and* the slave-owners are destined to be a marginal element of the new America. It'll be a whole new New World!" Justin snickered. "Now, there are still quite a few people in our organization who really are True Believers in human equality and the benefits of throwing all kinds of disparate human elements together. Lenin called people like that 'useful idiots.' They actually imagine that even though different kinds of Englishmen couldn't live in the same country without a war of secession, we can take bunches of Muslim Arabs, Hindus, Catholic Mexicans, and sub-Saharan tribals who are killing one another as we speak, throw them all on the soil of North America, and sing Kumbaya!

"Those guys are in the sociology end mostly, but just remember, if you're a gamer like me and your eyes are wide open, you have to be careful what you say around the True Believers. We need them. They have an emotionally-driven, religious-like fervor that makes them rather formidable. Oh, yeah, they're like harpies! Just make sure you don't say anything that will make them go after *you*! When you're writing—but hey, you're a pro; so you already know this—those are the ones you want to write for. They can't know, and they won't *let* themselves know, that the real game is creating conflict and then managing it. Do you have kids? No? Probably smart. But if you did, I'd say tell them the future is in managing diversity. We're talking trillions of dollars here. Mark my word. Consultants, translators, lawyers, security services, think about it!"

"Wow, yeah," said Dylan. "I see what you mean."

"Thanks, Justin," said Black, stepping back in from the hall, where he had been checking messages on his phone.

"Sure," answered Justin, who had already turned back to his computer without another word to Dylan. "Oh, geez, what's this from California? Ho, Ho! *¡La Reconquista!*"

Back in the elevator, Dr. Black remarked, "He's a bit on the Asperger's side. You won't find everyone here quite so," and he hesitated in search of the right word, "quite so *ruthlessly strategic* in their thinking, or quite so forthright in expressing it. He has absolutely no filter, *and* he's a genius! I suppose that's why the Chair always consults him on the more challenging decisions."

The elevator stopped, and the doors opened. To their left were the open doors of the boardroom, suffused with light from the northern sky. The rain had stopped, and shreds of gray and purple cloud scudded above the tree line.

"Ah! Finally! Are you as tired of being inside as I am?" exclaimed Black. "Come on, let's check out the grounds."

They walked quickly down the gray corridor, through the center of the old farm house, and out into a freshly washed landscape. "This way," said Black, and they turned to the right and followed a gravel path that curved past a mossy stone wall. "This was the foundation of the original barn, circa 1790. The house you see today was built half a century later." They continued along the path, which ran uphill along the southern end of the barn foundation.

"You'll stay a couple of days to get oriented, of course," remarked Black.

"A couple of days! I have a job!"

"No worries there. I've been in touch with your boss. He's only too happy to have an inside line to the Global Outreach. You've just become his most valuable employee."

Dylan felt his head swimming. What had he gotten himself into? He looked around. To his left, a little stream ran out of a stone building and into a pond. Beyond that was another pond with a gazebo. Ahead of him on the path, a peacock strutted.

"I've got to call my wife," he said. "Oh, wait, I don't have any clean clothes or anything!"

Armand Black laughed. "I'm sure that can all be arranged. We have heads of state, senators, billionaires, and movie stars as guests here. You'll find clean clothes in your room. I don't think you fully appreciate where you are. This is the center of everything that is happening, the home of the thought leaders for the thought leaders. One might even say the high temple of our secular religion."

They watched a pair of mallards fly off the lawn and onto the farthest pond.

"The other day I binge-watched a series called 'The Tu-dors.' Have you seen it?" asked Black.

"Yes, a while ago."

"I thought they chose too scrawny a fellow to play Henry VIII, but I was very impressed by the portrayal of Sir Thomas More. Here's the point, though. Picture the scene: Thomas More has it all. He's in the king's good graces; he's Lord Chancellor. Big estate, beautiful family. All he has to do, *all he has to do* is sign a paper, the Oath of Succession. Whether he does or doesn't won't change the course of events for Eng-land, but it can save his own life and the fortunes of his family. What does he do? He stands on principle and gets his head chopped off. Does that make any sense to you?"

Dylan shrugged.

"Nor to me. He martyred himself for nothing. Have a look at this. Isn't it beautiful?" The historian stopped beside the spring house, and the two men paused to admire the stonework and listen to the gurgling of the water. "I have no intention of choosing the losing side in a battle where the outcome is a fore-gone conclusion. I'm fifty-nine years old. I've got thirty years left, maybe. No children to worry about. The history of the world is one long succession of waves of invasion and exter-mination. I see the next wave coming, and I'm going to ride it. The principled losers can stand athwart it, yelling stop; but when they're seven fathoms under, I'll be riding the crest."

Chapter 9

Sidney read the text message resignedly. Dylan was going to stay at GOOD headquarters for a couple of days. "So, what else is new?" she said to herself. Sunday was her day to tidy up the apartment, and she was enjoying being alone, in her own private place. Still, though she would have denied keeping score, Dylan owed her for this one.

Half a block down the street was a Chinese restaurant. She phoned in her order. Twenty minutes later, she stood behind the counter, looking up at back-lit images of items on the menu. It was obvious that the success of the restaurant did not depend on the visual appeal of those dishes. All the pictures had faded to a pale, yellowish hue. The building rattled as a city bus pounded over the potholes just outside. A homeless man with wild eyes and a long, gray beard peered through the window for a moment, then moved on, shouting obscenities. Sidney paid for her meal, snatched up the plastic bag, and hurried home.

After organizing her teaching material for the next day, she took a long bath and went to bed early. In an instant, she was asleep.

She had the sensation of watching a period movie, but somehow, she was *in* it. The action was taking place all around her: noise of passing carriages, dust, tobacco smoke, and the pervasive smell of horse dung. Ahead of her, a small crowd gathered around a gaudily painted wagon. A wide awning extended from the front of the wagon, and from its leading edge hung a sign: Dent's Medical Emporium. A salesman in a top hat and frock coat was extolling the virtues of something called Dent's Gargling Oil and Liniment. There seemed to be nothing it couldn't cure. He had a remarkably strong voice, and he needed it. Sidney had always imagined that city streets were quieter before the days of automobiles. She had never before heard wagon wheels on gravel and paving stones.

A man was standing almost at her left elbow. As she turned to look at him, he politely inclined his head and tipped his hat. He was all in black, with a thin moustache; and like her, he stood a little back from the rest of the audience. A most peculiar creature was approaching him from his left. Bent almost double and clad in colorful robes, it wore a silken turban and carried a leather-bound box under its left arm. In its right hand was a carved staff with which it clawed its way forward. Its face was like the leather binding of the box, but more wrinkled, and its long, gray beard was streaked with brown and yellow. Drawing close to the gentleman in black, it said something in a language that Sidney did not understand.

"Parsee?" asked the gentleman.

The weird old man nodded and contorted his face into a toothless rictus.

"Sir, I fear I am almost entirely unschooled in your tongue. *Votre langue m'est inconnue, Monsieur.*"

The Parsee drew closer and said, "*J'ai ici c' que vous cherchez,*"[1] as his wizened fingers fumbled open the latch of the box he carried. Within, padded in scarlet silk, lay two small bottles filled with dark liquid. "*Vous craignez la nuit du tombeau! Ah! Que j'n'ai pas tort! Si! Enseveli sous terre, personne n'écoute vos cris. Mourir comme ça, tout seul. Chose affreuse!*"[2]

The gentleman's dark eyes widened with horror. He nodded mechanically. The Parsee jabbered faster and less intelligibly. He seemed to be promising that if, through some all-too-common medical error, you woke up to find yourself buried alive, the potion in the bottles would "cast you up free among the stars" or some such. Half a dollar a bottle. The

---

[1] I have here that which you seek.
[2] You fear the night of the tomb! Ah! I'm not mistaken! Yes! Buried under earth, no one hears your cries. To die like that, all alone. Frightful thing!

gentleman, as if in a trance, produced a silver dollar, put one bottle in each of his coat pockets, and walked away.

As the hunchback closed the leather box, the box grew larger and became a trunk, rectangular, with rounded corners and studded iron bands around it. Still it grew until it was an iron-bound desk of Oriental design, the same shade of brown but made of coarsely-grained wood. The bottles, the *same* bottles, stood on the desk, their red seals reflecting candle-light. And behind the desk sat a small, thick man in a wheel-chair, whose eyes, at first focused far away, shifted and looked into Sidney's own; and as they did, they seemed to become empty holes in a horrid mask.

She ran from the mask, down a gray corridor that went on forever; and as she ran, she knew the mask was following her.

Panting and drenched with sweat, she kicked off the blankets and switched on a light beside the bed. She wished Dylan were home. Then she decided that she was glad he was away. He'd only have thought she was crazy.

At the end of the bed was her great-great-grandmother's blanket chest. She opened it and gently lifted out a patchwork quilt. Its cheerful, multicolored pattern always reminded her of her childhood. Even the faint smell of mothballs was com-forting. She was an adult now, and she could stand up for her-self. But the quilt was what she needed at the moment. The night was chill. Sliding her feet into her fuzzy yellow slippers, she wrapped the quilt around her. Then she padded into the living room and curled up in an upholstered chair.

The clock-radio woke her with a weather report: warm and sunny, high 68. Despite the disturbing dream, she felt rested. The coffee tasted good this morning. Traffic was unusually light on her way to the college. This was going to be a good day. She was at peace with the world.

As usual, she checked her mail slot on the way to her office. It contained a flyer announcing a presentation called "White Privilege: Unpacking the Invisible Knapsack," to be held at the auditorium. Stapled to the flyer was a memo strongly advising faculty members to attend. There was also an official-looking envelope addressed to her. She tore it open with a growing sense of dread.

Dear Ms. Morgan-Greene:

You are receiving this letter because a grievance has been filed against you with the Office of Student Affairs. A hearing has been scheduled for 4:30 pm on Monday, April —, —— in Room 241 of the Administration Building. Failure to appear at the hearing will be grounds for disciplinary action.

This campus has a zero-tolerance policy for insulting, intolerant, or defamatory statements. Your conduct reflects on the college as a whole, and strict compliance with policy guidelines is required as a condition of continued employment.

Sincerely,

La'quan Jordan
Deputy Director of Student-Faculty Relations

Sidney could feel her heart pounding. She forced herself to breathe deeply. The rest of the day was a blur.

Exactly at 4:30, she knocked on the door of Room 241. A voice inside said, "Enter." She opened the door to find a table across the back of the room. Five women were seated at the table, facing her. Their backs were to the window, so that their faces were partly obscured by the glare of the declining sun. Nevertheless, Sidney could make out that all of them were, and she reproached herself for noticing, African-American.

"You may sit down," said the one in the middle. "I am Ms. Jordan. "Please state your name for the committee."

Sidney's mouth was dry. She shaded her eyes with her left hand. "Sidney Morgan-Greene," she replied.

"Ms. Morgan-Greene, we have received a serious complaint about your actions toward students in your class. Do you understand?"

"I understand what you are saying, but I don't know what the complaint is."

Ms. Jordan picked up a paper and read from it as if it had an offensive odor. "Item one: You spoke in favor of discrimination."

Sidney wondered whether she had heard correctly. Then she remembered what she had said. Of course! This was just a silly misunderstanding, and these ladies would see it immediately. Relieved, she gave a little, nervous laugh.

"So, you think this is funny? You think discrimination is a laughing matter?"

Sidney's smile disappeared. "Oh, no, of course not. No, I just laughed because this is nothing more than a misunderstanding. You see, I was telling the class that they needed to recognize the difference, that is to say, to *discriminate* between facts and opinions, between fictional accounts in historical novels and real documented accounts in legitimate histories. I…"

"So, you *did* say 'discriminate.' The complainants allege that you, and I *quote*, 'told the students that they need to *learn to discriminate.*' And you admit that."

There was a silence as the other committee members scribbled on their pads of paper. Sidney was at a loss. Had she not explained herself?

Could she say anything more on the subject without appearing argumentative?

"Item two, that you told one of the complainants that she should think about chains. About *chains!*"

A cloud had passed over the sun, and Sidney could see more clearly the face of her accuser. It was a fat, scowling face, and the wattles under the chin quivered with indignation. "Do you know, do you *know*, Ms. (and she looked at her papers) Morgan-Greene, *do you know* what that kind of language means to my people?"

The other committee members were shaking their heads and intoning "Mm-mm."

"My people, *our* people, were *brought* here in chains, and you just throw a word like that around like we be nothin' to you!"

The others took up the refrain, "Mm, mm. Nothin' to you."

"Now wait a minute," protested Sidney. "You're taking my words completely out of context. There's nothing wrong with what I said, and there is no way that any reasonable person should be offended by it. I was trying to get across the concept of logical connection, *linking* of one concept to another."

"So now you saying we are not reasonable?" asked Ms. Jordan angrily. "Is that what you saying?"

Sidney realized that that was exactly what she was saying. And thinking.

"Item three, you wrote on an essay written by one of the complainants, and I quote, 'Wakanda is not reality.'"

Sidney's head was spinning. Could these people be for real? "If I remember correctly," she offered, "what I wrote was, 'If you want to establish that European colonization prevented the emergence of more advanced civilization in Africa, argue from reality, from fact. Wakanda is not reality.'"

Ms. Jordan glared. "So, you disrespect the idea that people of color could create a place like Wakanda."

Sidney stood up. She felt as if she were outside her own body, a spectator at some bizarre theatre. "I'm leaving," she announced.

"I don't recall giving you permission to leave," said Ms. Jordan.

"I don't recall asking," replied Sidney, and she walked out and closed the door.

Dylan's phone was set to vibrate, but in the quiet of the library at GOOD headquarters, it emitted an audible buzz.

"Go ahead, answer it," said Dr. Black cheerily. "No need to be shy. You're among friends."

Dylan checked the display. To his intense irritation, Sidney's name appeared. They had an agreement that she would not call him at work except in case of emergency. He answered with a curt "Hello."

"I'm sorry to call you on a business trip, but I just had a horrible day." She had not felt like crying until this moment, but now she sobbed as she spoke. "It was like an inquisition! I waited till I got home before trying to call, but I have to talk to you. I don't know what to do. I think they're going to fire me!"

"Oh, now, it can't be that bad. Slow down. I'm having trouble understanding you."

Sidney was standing in the kitchen of the apartment. She had drunk a glass of Chardonnay and poured another before making her call. Now she took another sip and forced herself to recount the day's events.

"So, you just walked out? Damn. I can't believe you did that!"

"What was I supposed to do? Everything I said was wrong as far as they were concerned! They were out to get me from the beginning!" She began crying again. "You're supposed to be on *my* side!"

Dylan had set down his cocktail and walked to the far end of the library. He looked back to where he and Armand Black had been sitting in leather armchairs by the fire. Black had retreated to one of the huge walnut bookcases and opened a book, which he was making a pretense of reading.

"*Of course* I'm on your side," said Dylan, with growing embarrassment. "Look, I'm not really in a good place to talk. Maybe you could make an apology. Hello? Hello?" He looked at the phone. Disconnected.

"Problem?" asked Black.

"I think she hung up on me," said Dylan incredulously. "She's very upset about something that happened at work." Black made sympathetic noises and asked for details. It seemed more awkward to withhold the story than to tell it. After all, he thought, it was his wife's *faux pas*, not his.

The historian listened intently. "So, she walked out on them, eh? Well, it probably makes no difference to the outcome." He shook his head. "Too bad. This could cost her her career, at least in the public school system. And it will be on her record if she applies to teach at a private college."

"What can we do?" asked Dylan, with a feeling of doom. He began mentally calculating how they could manage without her income.

"Well, I think we can make this go away. We're dealing with a bureaucracy. The committee's report will go to someone who will decide what to do with it. All we need to do is persuade that individual to throw it in the trash. I'll see what can be done."

"Oh, man, that would be great! Thank you!"

Black waved his hand. "Don't thank me yet. Oh! Look, it's time for dinner."

The two left the library and crossed the central hall of the house. A spacious dining hall occupied the entire eastern end of the first floor. There was a polished walnut table with seating for at least sixteen, but only the lawyer Wheedler was there. He had helped himself and was already eating.

On a sideboard were plates, napkins, silverware, and four chafing dishes, containing rice, beef bourguignon, steamed broccoli, and dinner rolls. Wine glasses and cabernet sauvignon had been placed on a wheeled tea cart. When they had loaded their plates and seated themselves, Black proposed a toast, "Here's to having the right connections."

*C*hapter 10

Until Sidney's phone call, Dylan had been having one of the best days of his life. After a late evening sipping single-malt Scotch and hearing Armand (he insisted on being called by his first name) recount his adventures unearthing priceless antiquities in the Levant and detecting clever artistic forgeries at the Louvre, he had spent a restful night in an opulent bed chamber usually reserved for foreign dignitaries.

Next morning, he had been invited to shadow a very attractive young paralegal who was gathering documents from a translator. Her assignment was to prepare a position paper for the Supreme Court in support of substituting foreign legal precedents for American constitutional law. She was named Miguelina Gonzales, and she had large brown eyes and long black hair.

"This presentation isn't a formal *amicus curiae* brief. It's more like a crib sheet for the justices who see things the way we do. As you know, the U.S. constitution is an outmoded document that simply doesn't allow the flexibility that a modern government has to have in order to do everything it needs to do.

"You've probably read the op-eds lamenting that China is so far ahead of this country in being able to put new plans in motion without running into congressional obstructionism or legal challenges. Well, we're at the forefront of feeding the progressive justices the kind of information about foreign law that they need to basically paper-over the constitution.

"Most of Europe has eliminated the so-called Freedom of Speech with regard to protected minorities and victim groups, especially Muslims and asylum-seekers from Africa. We can't quite do that here. Some people we can isolate or silence by the usual accusations of 'white supremacism.' We can pressure employers, advertisers, big businesses in general, into suppressing trouble makers, but we can't yet arrest somebody for criticizing Muslim immigration, the way they can in France. We really need more robust legal sanctions, and that's what we're working on.

"The new international law institute downtown will give us a huge boost. Imagine having a building full of the best progressive legal minds with access to all the best info! And translators! Do you know what a drag it is to wait for translations when you're not sure the text in question is going to be useful?"

"So, basically what you're about is the abolition of the

United States of America as we know it," said Dylan.

Miguelina pouted charmingly. "At GOOD, we prefer the term 'radical transformation,' but I kind of like the way you put it. It's a logical progression from abolition of slavery to the abolition of the white European culture that allowed slavery to flourish in the first place. You ought to write a piece for your paper suggesting that. No wonder they say you're such a good writer. Have you considered going into law?"

Dylan had always thought of himself as a First Amendment guy. Freedom of the press is kind of important if you're in the press corps. But he had already accepted the restrictive speech code at his college, and he believed that some ideas are too dangerous to discuss. For example, if you let the average slob get hold of the notion that race and gender differences are biologically-based, there's no telling what he'll do! From that perspective, it's not much of a leap to abandon free speech entirely and turn the whole messy business over to wise and impartial officials of the government. Besides, he really liked this chick.

He and Miguelina ate lunch together in the employee cafeteria. It was like being back in college and solving the problems of the world. Except that these guys really *were* solving the problems of the world.

After lunch, Mr. Wheedler came to introduce Dylan to the director of the Smart Chip initiative. Chuck Yu had a round Asian face and wore a white lab coat. He spoke without an accent.

"I understand your background is in biomedical engineering," said Dylan.

"Yes, that's right, with an emphasis on development of connectivity between communication and power-assist devices and the human central nervous system."

"You mean like bionic limbs?"

"Oh, far beyond that. I'm more interested in the enhancement of human intelligence. Imagine if you could find any piece of information you wanted just by thinking of it. Then pair that with a super-genius-level artificial intelligence system, and we humans become practically a whole new species. It's the long-awaited Singularity, the quantum-jump in human consciousness.

"We are incredibly close to making that jump. Do you know that in Palo Alto, there's a robot on just about every corner, observing humans, learning, absorbing, putting together patterns? These robots listen to every conversation. They recognize and remember faces and voices and link them together. All the information they gather is shared, so that when one learns, all learn. Each robot is autonomous, but because of information-sharing, there are as many back-up data copies as there are robots.

"We're doing the same kind of thing with the surveillance cameras in Baltimore. They're crude, really primitive compared to the Palo Alto program, but here we'll collect data in three stationary artificial minds. Which brings me to the chip project, and you are the first member of the press to get the real inside scoop on this."

Dylan nodded and said, "I appreciate that."

"Our goal is to get every American citizen chipped within five years. Now, when I say citizen, that doesn't include resident aliens, etcetera. Our legal team feels that chipping immigrants, especially undocumented ones, might violate their rights; so, we're not doing that."

"What about the rights of American citizens?" asked Dylan.

Mr. Yu laughed. "Hey, I'm an engineer, not a lawyer. GOOD has lots of lawyers. They're experts in *their* field, so I do what they say. Anyway, the program is voluntary, at least in Phase One. That's what we need to promote. The first thousand people who sign up will get the chip implanted for free. The rest will pay a nominal fee, and we expect grant money for the underprivileged."

"What about after Phase One?"

"Have you noticed that everybody today has a cell phone and usually at least one computer? Nobody forced them to buy those, right? But you can't function without them in today's world. It'll be the same with the chip. Today a convenience, tomorrow a necessity. Have you visited our currency department? Well, the director is here, but the real action is at the D.C. office. We're working toward eliminating cash money. When cash becomes illegal, you'll have to have either a card or a chip. And the functionality of the card may, shall we say, degrade, as every business, bank, and government office invests in the latest chip reader but has trouble maintaining the older technology.

"And when we roll out the mind-enhancement series, *everybody* will line up for a chip. Imagine what a disadvantage it would be to compete for a job with someone who could instantly access all the information *and* process it faster than a human brain! That's why we're doing sub-occipital insertions right from the outset, so we refine placement of the device to communicate directly with the brain.

"But see for yourself. Here, come through into the lab. Look through this window; we're putting a chip in a volunteer."

In a small medical procedure room, a man lay face down on a padded steel table, with his head bent forward and resting in a hollow. He was covered with a sheet except for his head and neck. A strap had been placed across the back of his head, and a technician was shaving the nape of his neck just below the skull.

"Is he under anesthesia?" asked Dylan.

"Uh, well, just heavily sedated. Actually, I think this subject is technically not a volunteer. He was brought in by Captain Bollard. She said something about him being an escape risk."

The tech swabbed the shaved spot with a clear liquid, then prepared an injection.

"That'll be the local anesthetic. Then a small incision, three or four millimeters, and..."

The tech inserted a thick needle through the incision, pressed a blue plastic handle on the needle, and pulled it back out. A small red puddle of blood appeared, and he held a gauze pad in place until the bleeding stopped.

"There you are. Chip inserted! Five minutes of compression is usually sufficient," said Yu.

Two green-uniformed officers entered the procedure room and pulled the sheet off, revealing that the man was strapped to the table. They released all the straps and pulled him into a sitting position, facing the window, which was apparently a one-way mirror. One of the officers, oblivious to the observers, was looking straight into the mirror, smoothing his hair and straightening his uniform. When he stepped aside, the subject's face came into view. Dylan's mouth dropped open. He had seen this face before. The drowsy patient was the missing person he had read about in the news.

He took care to conceal his surprise and his instinctive suspicion that something was amiss. Livvy Bollard and her green-clad cops made him profoundly uncomfortable, but perhaps, he thought, that discomfort arose from his own unconscious prejudice against women in positions of authority.

There had to be a reasonable explanation. GOOD was devoted to the welfare of humankind. Therefore, what he had just witnessed was clearly an appropriate and beneficent act. Here was a fellow who must be a few cards short of a deck, who ran away and distressed his family. Now they had a way to keep track of his whereabouts. End of story. Reason triumphs over prejudice.

"I understand that you'll be writing about the chip program," said Yu. "The right presentation is so important in getting the public to cooperate. We have our in-house writers, but you, as an esteemed member of the press, have much more credibility. You have no axe to grind. Fair and balanced, as they say.

"I'm not a wordsmith, and I'm not a policy-maker, so I probably haven't given you the best outline of the program and its potential. Let me introduce you to the creative team. They're on the next floor up."

By the time he joined Armand for drinks in the elegant Global Outreach Library, Dylan was exhausted but more pleased with his prospects than he had been for a long time. All these people were making him feel important, and the creative team had practically written three great articles for him. They didn't even want credit. Somewhere in the back of his mind, a little voice was asking whether uncritical publication of some organization's advertising was entirely ethical, but he was confident in his own independent judgment and dismissed the little voice's quibbles.

Chapter 11

Tuesday morning, Sidney slept late. She had no classes scheduled that day. As she clattered about in the kitchen, she was surprised that the dreams of the last two nights still intruded vividly on her mind, so unlike her usual dreams, which faded away like smoke. Without any definite plan, she took her mug of coffee, padded downstairs in her slippers, and knocked on the Fitzgeralds' door.

"Coming!" called Rose. The door opened, and the kindly face of the landlady appeared. "Good morning, my dear, would you like some toast to go with your coffee?"

Sidney had no strong desire for toast, but she needed time to warm up before talking. "Yes, thank you," she replied.

The two women sat down at a small table in the breakfast room, a sunny little space off the south side of the kitchen. The cozy room, hot toast, butter, marmalade, and coffee gave Sidney a feeling of safety, and she realized how much she had missed that feeling.

"Rose, could you tell me more about Wanda?"

"Of course, dear. Wanda is from Virginia. She is a very bright lady, with advanced degrees in economics and business. In fact, she used to be high up in the Securities and Exchange Commission. Then she became ill. The doctors informed her that she had fourth stage uterine cancer and that she was going to die. So, she went to see a Reiki master, figuring that she had nothing to lose and might as well try alternative medicine.

"The Reiki therapist told her, 'You don't need me. *You* are a healer. You can heal yourself.'

"And she did just that. She healed herself. Fifteen years later, she's still around, and she has organized a ministry and devoted herself to healing others. She met and married her husband Paul shortly before the doctors told her that she would die."

"I think I may have seen him at her farm. Is he a big man with red hair and a moustache and goatee?"

"And a bit overdressed for a farmer? Yes, that's the man. Paul is an interesting character, an attorney. He used to work for Baltimore City, but they fired him."

"Why?"

"He opposed the removal of the Confederate monuments. When he addressed the city council, he explained that he 'didn't have a dog in this fight.' His grandparents came over from Scandinavia around 1900. What concerned him was that the city government was going to tear down precious shrines that are dear to the memory of Baltimoreans past and present. He said it was as if a bunch of anti-Semites were proposing to demolish the Holocaust Memorial on Lombard Street. Even though he personally thought the memorial was ugly and depressing and had nothing to do with him, he would oppose its destruction with every fiber of his being. Why? Because it's sacred to part of our community. You destroy that, it's like vandalizing a church because you don't agree with the religion, or like knocking over somebody's gravestone because he treated you badly when he was alive. Attacks on memorials, he said, destroy the cohesion of a community. They destroy trust. Nothing is sacred, and nothing is safe. Whose temple will be violated next? He called the removal of the statues a crime against the community and a sacrilege. He concluded, if I remember correctly, with these words, 'You, in your ignorance and your petty, tribal vindictiveness, have no idea what furies this desecration will unleash!'

"He says that they just sat there, stony-faced. Then they fired him. He even lost his pension. And the *Herald* ran a hit piece twisting his words and calling him an anti-Semite and (can you guess?) a white supremacist."

"Do you think he is?"

"What? Well, I'm not sure I know what a white supremacist is, other than someone those people want to shut up.
Paul was a 1960's radical who marched with Martin Luther
King in Selma. He believes what King is generally thought
to have believed, that the same laws should apply to everybody regardless of race. Then, over the years, Paul saw the
dream of equal treatment under the law replaced by the nightmare of racial preferences, with whole cities desolated by
court-ordered busing and the white flight that followed. He
felt that the civil rights movement had been perverted by
power-mad judges who had lost touch with reality. For him,
that was the end of the Dream."

"Speaking of dreams," Sidney said, "I've had two more
since I went out to see Wanda." She described her vision of
a man who looked like pictures she had seen of Edgar Allan
Poe, how he had bought potions from a strange bearded man
in a turban, and how the potions had reappeared on the desk
of the cruel old man in the wheelchair, whose face became a
horrid mask that pursued her down an endless corridor. Rose
listened carefully, nodding as if the dream made some kind
of sense.

"Then last night," Sidney continued, "I was looking over
the shoulder of a frail man with a full beard. He coughed
frequently, and he wrote by the light of an oil lamp. He was
muttering, "Evan Fitzgerald, dear me, how long since the

pleasant old days in Baltimore!" I saw that he was addressing a letter to your husband; but the date was impossible, 1873, I think. His handwriting was old-fashioned too, with some of his s's written like f's. He put a slip of blue paper, sort of a cornflower blue with numbers on it, in with the letter. Then the letter sprouted wings and became a bird and flew away and landed on the front porch of *this house*, and a big police woman in a green uniform grabbed the bird by the neck and squeezed it. Oh, it was disgusting to see her squeeze it so. She turned around, and right behind her was the wicked old man in the wheelchair, who took the bird and ate it whole!"

"I think we should call Wanda," said Rose.

At the same moment, Dylan was enjoying a sumptuous breakfast at GOOD headquarters with Armand Black. Just as he was helping himself to some more eggs Benedict, his phone vibrated. It was his friend Glen at the *Herald*.

"Dylan! Hello, can you hear me?" Glen was shouting into the phone. There was some sort of commotion in the background.

"Yes. What's the matter? Where are you?"

"Where am I? *I'm* at the *office*. You know, the rat race, the old grind? The question is, where the hell are *you*, buddy? Jack Grimmes is having a fucking hysterical *shit fit*!" Glen held up the phone receiver in the direction of Jack.

The senior editor was prancing up and down the office with his hands in the air. He wore a purple crushed-velvet jacket, a golden-yellow silk shirt with a burgundy ascot, charcoal trousers, and black loafers with tassels. Every time he passed by his own desk, he would pick up a handful of papers, wave them around for emphasis, and then toss them into the air, so that the floor was now littered with photographs, real estate advertisements, and even a few personal letters on colorful stationery.

"Oh! Oh!" he wailed, fanning himself with a realtor's flyer, "This is *too* impossible! I think I'm going to faint! No, no, I'm going to go utterly, *utterly* insane! Where *is* that *outrageous* boy? My world is in chaos! Water! I need water! No, I need a real drink, an adult libation! Blessed ethanol, restorative spirits! My nerves are shattered! *Au revoir, mes amis!* I shall return anon, when I have recovered my strength. *Down, down I go, glistering Phaeton, wanting the manage of unruly jades!*"

Glen put the phone back to his own ear. "Well, he just fluttered out of the office. Probably off to the Drinkery. You'd better get your ass back here, if it's not already too late!"

Looking pointedly at Black, Dylan said, "Honestly, Glen, I was assured that GOOD had contacted the boss and that he had approved my absence."

Armand Black shrugged and held out his palms in the universal sign for "Beats me. I thought it was handled."

"Listen, Glen, thanks for calling. I'm on my way. For God's sake tell the boss I'm on my way!" Dylan pressed the end-call button. Then he remembered that he had left his car in the downtown garage and ridden out in Armand's BMW.

"Sorry if there's been an upset," said Black, blotting his mouth and laying the napkin on the table. "May I offer you a ride to work?"

They were on the road in a matter of minutes. Dylan was trembling with anxiety for his job and taut with anger at the whole pompous, powerful, profligate project of GOOD. They had been toying with him, he thought, flattering him so that he would write what they wanted him to write.

"For what it's worth, you made a favorable impression on the staff out there," remarked Armand after driving for twenty minutes in silence. "I shouldn't be surprised if they weren't having a discussion about possibly bringing you on board. That is, if you were interested. The illusion of independent journalism is so completely shattered today that on reflection, we really don't think you'd be any more credible or effective recycling our press releases through the *Herald* than you would be writing them for us to disseminate through *all* the news outlets. If you worked for us, you'd be more directly involved in the creative process, and you could stay focused on the topics that matter instead of squandering your talents on puff pieces for real estate. And I can't imagine you'd mind a pay raise."

Dylan abruptly revised his uncharitable assessment of the Global Outreach, but he cautioned himself not to appear over-eager. After as long a pause as he could manage, he said, "I'd be open to an offer."

"Well, we shall see. Of course, there *are* a few formalities. The Chair is very particular about knowing the *character* of the people we hire, and it's customary to conduct informal interviews. I've already taken the liberty of sounding out your boss at the newspaper. One more character reference would do. I don't suppose you could arrange for me to meet with your landlord, what was his name?"

"Oh, Dr. Evan Fitzgerald."

"Ah yes, just so. The fourth of that name! Perhaps some evening this week?" As the BMW pulled up in front of Dylan's office tower, Armand drew a couple of business cards from a leather case in the glove box. "When you see him this evening, hand him one of these and tell him that if he doesn't mind, I'll be giving him a call."

Armand Black detested the basement of the GOOD headquarters. In the course of his archaeological work, he had crept through catacombs, crawled through crevices and even splashed through sewers, without a qualm. But the grim security office with its steel grill always sent a chill down his spine.

Captain Bollard was waiting for him in her office. She was admiring an array of handcuffs and shackles on her desk. "Come in, *Professor*," she said, "and close the door. The Chair is anxious to get hold of the coded message. He told me to make sure that you weren't dawdling."

There was something between mockery and disdain in the way Bollard always pronounced the word "Professor," and Black replied in kind. "Is that so, *Captain*? Do you think you can get what we're after by arresting Fitzgerald and putting the thumb screws to him? I can manage quite well, thank you, without the clumsy interference of your enforcers. This week, I expect to have a private chat with the good doctor; and if he has the letter, I'm confident that he'll want to share it for the sake of historical accuracy."

Livvy Bollard maintained a thin-lipped smile as she stood up and walked around her desk. She picked up a shiny, black truncheon from amidst the assortment of gear that covered almost her entire work-surface. In her police boots, she stood a head taller than the professor; and she stepped up close in front of him, first slapping the truncheon on her left palm and then sliding it back and forth between her left thumb and forefinger. "Try it your way, Prof," she whispered, "and when *you* come up empty, *I'll* be ready. There's no time to waste. Chambers thinks the Chair has had another attack of some kind. He says the old man is convinced that the end is near."

She pressed the club against the center of the professor's chest. "Make sure you let me know *immediately* after you meet with Fitzgerald."

Dylan slogged up the cellar stairs at seven in the evening. He proceeded through the first-floor hall and opened the front door with the intention of checking the mailbox. Out on the front porch was Dr. Fitzgerald, watering a box of red geraniums that hung on the railing. At the sound of the door, he turned around and said, "Good evening. Long day?"

Dylan nodded. "It was a rough one. I was away on Monday, and when I came back, my senior editor was really put out. I wound up cramming at least two days' work into one." Opening the lid of the mailbox, he found it empty. "I guess Sidney must have already picked up the mail," he mumbled.

"It's in the nature of things," opined the doctor, "that we pay for our time off. It would be the same even if you worked for yourself. So, you played truant yesterday. Where did you go?"

"I spent some time at GOOD headquarters, up in northern Baltimore County. They're talking about offering me a job."

"What do you really know about this organization?"

"Oh, well, they are working on many different fronts, promoting diversity and race-and-gender equity and encouraging the American judicial system to adopt a more flexible approach toward application of transnational legal precedents. And they're also on the verge of opening up a whole range of exciting advances using embedded computer chips to make everybody's life easier and safer, and ultimately, to enhance the power of the human brain! I guess you could say they're into everything!"

Dr. Fitzgerald frowned. "And you approve of what they're doing?"

Dylan thought back over his experiences at GOOD, the overbearing woman in charge of security, the computer nerd with Asperger's who had outlined a strategy of revolution through intentional creation of conflict between identity groups, the gorgeous Latina developing strategies to overthrow the Constitution, and the scientist putting a chip in the neck of a prisoner…no, a *patient*. There were some things that had been a little outside his comfort zone, but, hey!

"They're the future," said Dylan. "I'm sure there are parts of their program that you wouldn't agree with, but, well, I wouldn't want to be on the wrong side of history."

"That doesn't sound like a resounding endorsement to me. And you've given me no specifics, only the latest focus-group-approved buzz-words. I have a very bad feeling about this outfit, and everything I've read has reinforced that impression. Do you know who's behind the whole thing? Klaus Pyknos, the megalomaniac currency speculator and destroyer of economies. Now he's come for us, for America; and whatever nice slogans he may have, his intention is to divide and rule, to crush out the historic American nation, and to enslave the entire world."

Dylan stood for a moment with his mouth open. "Gee, that's a bit strong!"

"Open your eyes, Dylan. This is a guy who pays flash mobs to shut down anyone who tries to speak up against his program of destruction. This is a guy who promotes the demolition of beautiful and historically significant statues. Why, you've seen the empty pedestals yourself! This is third-world tribal revanchism. The vandal hasn't taken such a toll in an English-speaking country since Oliver Cromwell's roundheads smashed up the churches! If that's the future, Heaven help us! And you want to work for *them*? Good God!"

"I, uh, really haven't made my mind up. You obviously disapprove, and yeah, okay, I get that. I guess there wouldn't be any point in giving you as a character reference."

"You want *me* to tell *them* what I think of *your* character! Ha! That's like a gangster asking a headmaster to vouch for the ethical standards of one of his students! Well, it's them I disapprove of, not you, though I'm beginning to have my doubts. What do you need, a letter?"

"Actually," said Dylan, extracting Armand Black's card from his shirt pocket, "this gentleman said to ask you if you would be so kind as to give him a few minutes of your time. Like maybe some evening this week?"

Fitzgerald took the card. It bore the name "Armand Black, PhD," an address on a fashionable street in Roland Park, and a phone number with a 467 exchange. "Hopkins-7," muttered the doctor. "So, he lives just up the road, does he? And what is his position with GOOD?"

"He's a sort of historian and researcher and diplomat. I think he has a title of "liaison" of something or other. He doesn't seem to have an office of his own at GOOD headquarters."

"Well, Dylan, I feel that as the head of this household, I stand to some degree *in loco parentis* with respect to you and Sidney. In that capacity, I strongly advise you to steer clear of what I have every reason to believe is an evil enterprise. But I won't withhold my endorsement of your character, to the extent that I can attest to it under the circumstances. And I intend, for your sake, as well as for my own curiosity, to find out what I can about this fellow Black and his relationship to Pyknos.

"Yes, we'll see what the old devil's henchman has to say for himself. Tomorrow evening is the only time I have available this week. Let's do this: if you want to invite him to *your* apartment, I can come up and talk to him." He handed the card back to Dylan.

At that moment, Rose bustled out onto the porch. "Good evening, gentlemen," she said. "Dylan, you must excuse us, but I'm running late, and I'm sure Evan must be famished." She took her husband's hand and led him back into the house.

"No problem," Dylan called after them, but his words were lost in the noise of a passing truck. He stood in the dusk, in the grip of his habitual angst of being on the outside, looking in. Through the sheer curtains on the French doors, he watched the forms of the Fitzgeralds until they vanished into the back rooms of the house.

After ladling some chili from a crock pot, Rose handed Evan a full bowl, and the couple sat down at the dining table. "I went out to Wanda's today," Rose began. "Sidney came to me this morning with more of her dreams, and one of them concerned us."

She went on to repeat in detail all that Sidney had told her. "Wanda closed her eyes and sat still for several minutes. When she opened her eyes, she said that there must be a letter in your possession that Pyknos is desperate to acquire. She said that the Evil One has entered into his mind and soul 'eighty percent.' Well, I don't know how she gets this information, but she says it comes to her when she opens herself to the Source. And you know how precise she is about numbers.

"Anyway, Pyknos senses that he is dying, and both he and the diabolic entity that is moving into him are trying to acquire this letter, or rather something on blue paper enclosed with the letter. It seems that they believe the numbers on the blue paper are a clue that they need. Wanda said that if you have such a paper, you must destroy it lest it fall into their hands.

"She also said that a construction fence has gone up around Westminster Hall and the graveyard. She's been certain for some time that something important was going to happen at Poe's grave, and that the souls of the departed were about to be disturbed. That's why she sent Joe down there in January. He's kind of an idiot savant, and he sees dead people fairly often, without attaching any special significance to it. Wanda was hoping that he would notice any unusual paranormal activity and report back to her. Instead, Pyknos' people nabbed him."

"They've been holding him since January?" asked Evan. "Why?"

"*They* are trying to use him to get to Wanda. I hate to think what they've been doing to him. He's too loyal to talk, and his mind doesn't work like a normal person's."

"They could turn him loose and track him."

"Wanda instructed Joe *not* to return to her farm. He was to go to your medical office if he got into trouble."

"Great! When was she going to tell me *that*?" Dr. Fitzgerald paused to think. "If I hadn't known Wanda for so many years, I'd dismiss all this supernatural talk as utter nonsense. But I've sent a few hopeless cases to her, and they've come back completely healed, with wild descriptions of angelic beings or extraterrestrial surgeons operating on them in their sleep. So, I'm willing to accept that there are depths and heights of this reality to which I am oblivious. But what can Wanda do against Pyknos? Why would he or his demon want to *get to* her, as you put it?"

"Dear me," said Rose, "I have no idea, except that Wanda can call on powerful resources, as your own patients have attested. She's brave; she opposes them; and she's a factor they can't control. And isn't *control* what *they* are all about?"

Dr. Fitzgerald nodded. Snatching a stack of mail off the sideboard, he walked into his study, where he opened a file cabinet and withdrew a yellowed envelope. Opening it, he removed and unfolded a letter containing a piece of blue paper. With a pencil, he copied a series of numbers from the upper portion of the paper to the blank lower portion.

He thumbed through a dark-green, cloth-bound volume until he found the poem that he wanted:

> *It was many and many a year ago,*
> *In a kingdom by the sea,*

That a maiden there lived whom you may know
*By the name of **Annabel Lee**;*
And this maiden she lived with no other
thought
Than to love and be loved by me.

Carefully, he counted the letters in the poem, writing more numbers on the blue paper as he did so. Then he snipped the paper in half with a pair of scissors, putting the lower half with the new numbers back in the envelope with the letter and crushing the upper half of the blue paper into a ball. Among the day's mail, he found the latest form letter inviting him to join the American Medical Association. It was only lightly sealed, and he opened it carefully. Discarding the contents, he slipped the antique envelope inside, resealed it, and placed it under an unopened utility bill in a mahogany box marked "Incoming Mail."

When he rejoined his wife in the kitchen, he laid the small wad of blue paper with Poe's coded message in a ceramic bowl and lit a match. The paper burned brightly, with almost no smoke.

$\mathcal{C}$hapter 12

Wednesday morning, Sidney returned to work with a sick feeling in the pit of her stomach. The panel of inquisitors could not have been happy that she walked out on them, and Sidney was sure that they were plotting their revenge. She checked her mail box, but the only thing in it was a flyer announcing a White Privilege Walk, with a message from the Office of Diversity and Inclusion reminding faculty that if they missed the last one, they were required to attend this one. So, nothing unusual in the regular mail. Her email was similarly free of threatening communications, but the absence of information did not relieve her anxiety.

Dylan, too, returned to what outwardly appeared to be his old routine, but he wondered why he had not heard back from

Armand. After his conversation with Dr. Fitzgerald the night before, he had immediately sent a phone text inviting Armand to dinner. By two in the afternoon, with only five hours left until the dinner hour, Dylan sprang out of his chair and began pacing. He walked down to the break room and made a cup of hot cocoa. Just then, his cell phone rang. "Armand! Oh, that's okay. Yes. Great. See you then. I'll call Dr. Fitzgerald."

The rest of the day wore on slowly. Dylan's anxiety shifted from whether Armand was coming to whether he would be suitably impressed when he came. Sidney continued to wonder when the axe would fall, but by five o'clock, it had still not fallen.

On the way home, Dylan stopped in Little Italy to pick up some genuine spumoni for dessert, and Sidney visited Eddie's Supermarket, where she bought ready-made "shrimp scampi," a pre-packaged Caesar salad, and, for an appetizer, some little biscuits and a savory, salty spread made from real Smithfield ham.

Sidney had heard all about Armand Black, PhD, from Dylan. She reflected that in all the time she had known him, Dylan's choice of chums had never impressed her favorably. Glen she had met once, and he had been vulgar and shallow, just like the kids at college who played stupid pranks and persuaded

Dylan to get drunk. Armand was likely to be no better, she told herself; but when he arrived, precisely on time, she greeted him with as much cordiality as she could muster.

"What a pleasure to meet you," exclaimed Armand. "Your husband has been singing your praises without ceasing! You are a lucky couple!" His eyes darted appraisingly around the apartment. The furniture was all new, heavy and bulky, of honey-colored oak and ash, in a Chinese factory imitation of colonial style. There were no pictures on the walls. "Charming place," he said with a smile.

"I hope you like shrimp scampi," said Sidney nervously. Though she expected not to like this man, she did want to impress him.

"Tautological dishes are a favorite of mine," he replied. Now his beady eyes were fixed on her. She wore a thick, fuzzy sweater and a tartan skirt, and she was torn between being glad that she had dressed modestly and wishing she had been more daring. The man was a bit shifty, but he had style and wit.

The dinner went off flawlessly. The food was superb, and Armand engaged Sidney in discussions of literature and philosophy, asking for her opinions but never talking about himself. They had just retired to the living room when there was a knock at the door, and Dylan admitted Dr. Fitzgerald. After introductions, the doctor sat down across from Black.

"You wanted a character reference?"

Black smiled and shrugged as if mildly embarrassed. "One of those awkward formalities. Security concerns, you know. It's the modern age; nobody really knows anybody else anymore."

"Well, I can tell you that I've been acquainted with Dylan for about eight months now, and he pays the rent on time. As to whether he is who he says he is, if that's what you mean to ask, I have no way of knowing, beyond the fact that he passed the routine credit check and basic criminal background check that we run on all tenants. He and his wife are good neighbors and keep the place in good shape."

Black laughed nervously. "No more and no less than I expected. As I said, a formality. And do I understand correctly that you are a medical doctor? Internal medicine?"

"Yes. I'm one of the few remaining solo practitioners in Baltimore. And you, you are employed by Klaus Pyknos?"

"Ah, yes, I suppose you could say that. I do historical research and some community outreach for GOOD. Occasionally, I get involved in recruiting young talent for the organization. I've lived in Baltimore for only a few years, and I'm fascinated by its history. Your family goes way back in this town, right?"

"Yes, there were ancestors of mine here before Baltimore was a town."

"Very interesting. Did any of your family know H.L. Mencken? He must have been a character!"

"No, I'm afraid not."

"Ah, and then there's Poe. Now there's a brilliant writer, and his death remains such a mystery! I must confess to being a bit of a Poe enthusiast. I've done some research, but nobody seems to have any contemporaneous documents that shed any light on what really happened to him."

"That's why it's a mystery," replied Fitzgerald coolly.

"Hmm. I should have thought that such an eminent Baltimorean as yourself might have some, oh, I don't know, some family memorabilia or correspondence that might shed some light. No? Not even anything related to John R. Thompson?"

Fitzgerald raised his eyebrows. "John *Reuben* Thompson? Editor of the *Southern Literary Messenger*?"

Black nodded encouragingly.

"Odd that you should ask about him. He wasn't a Baltimorean. Interesting chap, though. It *is* a fact that like Poe's wife Virginia Clemm, he died of tuberculosis in the state of New York. He was a bit of a poet too, albeit not of the first rank. He wrote against Lincoln's plans to resort to force against the states that had seceded. The poem was entitled 'Coercion.'

"Could you conquer us, men of the North—
could you bring

199

Desolation and death on our homes as a flood—
Can you hope the pure lily, affection, will spring
From ashes all reeking and sodden with blood?"

"Hmm," said Black, "Just so. The advocates of peace haven't had much success in our history, have they? Oh, well. I suppose if I keep asking around, maybe someone with more extensive family records will be able to help me."

"Perhaps so. But tell me, Dr. Black, what sort of person is this Pyknos? To read some accounts, one would think he was the devil incarnate!"

"Ha! Well, you know what they say about believing everything you read. He stays out of the limelight, works behind the scenes. And he's immensely rich and powerful, so naturally people feel threatened and make up stories about him."

Dr. Fitzgerald stood up. "No doubt. Well, unless you have any other questions concerning our young man here, I'll wish you all a good night."

Armand Black remained standing after the doctor's footsteps had died away down the stairs. "You know, Dylan, I think it's time you met our Chair. Now that all the formalities have been dispensed with, that is. I'll email your boss. I'm sure he'll be cooperative. In case you don't remember the route, here's the address for your GPS navigation. We'll expect you at nine A.M. Your provisional ID badge will open the main gate. Sidney, *au revoir.*"

As soon as the door was closed and Black was safely out of earshot, Dylan grinned broadly, clenched his fists, and shouted, "Yes!"

"Congratulations, dear!" said Sidney.

"Can you believe Fitzgerald?" muttered Dylan. "He was as cold as ice. And he's fixated on stuff that happened 150 years ago."

"Well, you know he disapproves of GOOD and its projects. I think under the circumstances it was generous of him to talk to Armand at all."

"Maybe, but he had the nerve to lecture *me* yesterday evening as if I were a child, and *his* child at that! Well, now you'll get to see what it's like to be around people at the cutting edge of societal change, instead of backward-thinking old fogies like the Fitzgeralds."

Sidney frowned. She liked Rose, who had been much more understanding than her own husband lately. And Dr. Evan, well, she didn't know whether she agreed with him, but she admired his steadiness. "You shouldn't talk about them that way. They're good, kind people. And they have *integrity.*"

"And I don't?" asked Dylan angrily. "Here I am on the verge of landing a world-class position with a company headed by one of the richest people in the world, and all you can do is criticize me. How can you side with the Fitzgeralds against me? *Their kind* are on their way to extinction. They're being replaced."

"Can't I stand up for people who have befriended me without you taking it as a personal insult? And what do you mean *their kind*? What kind is that exactly? Normal, decent Americans? I'm beginning to think that's *just* what you mean, you and the people who are out to get me at school! Whose side are *you* on, anyway?"

Dylan put his hands up. "I'm *not* having this discussion, okay? I'm not." And he stalked back to the bedroom and slammed the door.

Chapter 13

Dylan arrived ten minutes early and stopped his car in one of a dozen unmarked parking spaces in front of the historic mansion that masked the front of GOOD headquarters. He bounded onto the wide veranda. The door opened, and he came face to face with Livvy Bollard. She was in full uniform, including a policeman's hat with a shiny black visor.

She smiled at his obvious discomfiture. "Expected your friend the Professor, no doubt," she purred. "He'll be busy today. You are to come with me." She walked quickly. "Too much sitting around, I see. Well, I can get your blood flowing," and she gripped his arm and hustled him down the gray corridor, around a corner, and into an elevator with a golden door that opened when she touched a Lucite panel. Dylan could see the subtle bump of the security chip under the skin on the back of her hand.

She pressed the button for the top floor. A bald man in a dark suit greeted them at a desk that faced the elevator. "Here we are, Chambers," said Bollard.

Chambers arose creakily. "The Chair will see you now," he announced, and led them through an enormous, heavy door of some exotic red wood, wrought with shapes of beasts and creeping things.

A small man sat behind a dark desk. He appeared as a silhouette against the bright picture window. His head tilted slowly from side to side, then abruptly righted itself. "You may go now, Chambers," he said. "Introduce us, Captain Bollard."

"Sir, allow me to present Dylan Greene, journalist. Mr. Greene, meet the Chair."

"It's an honor, sir," stammered Dylan.

"You are a *news*...paper-man," intoned the chair, drawing out the word news and leaving a pause after it, as if he were describing a species of man, made of paper. "You will know that I am Klaus Pyknos. I am a fair employer, and I demand neither more nor less than *absolute* loyalty and obedience. Do you understand me?"

"Yes, sir," replied Dylan.

"Good. You may go. Captain Bollard will give you your first assignment."

Dylan bowed involuntarily. As he turned toward the door, he started at the sight of the Samurai armor, which loomed to his right like a horned warrior from another world. In an instant, he regained his composure. "That was an easy interview," he thought, as he followed the captain back to the elevator.

Back on ground level, Bollard escorted him to a small, windowless office with a computer desk and a chair. "Sit," she ordered. She stood behind him with her hands heavy on his shoulders. "You are going to write an article praising the removal of Westminster Church and graveyard for construction of the World Justice Tower."

"By removal, you mean moving it all out to the county, right?"

"Oh, right, you can say that there is a *plan* to put all that old crap out at Druid Ridge, but you aren't writing about what happens to the *old*. You're pushing *transformation*. The relevant talking points are in the folder. Ring my extension when you're done."

At the same time that Dylan was typing his article, the Whiting-Turner Construction Company, with its famous efficiency, was completing the final sections of an eight-foot fence around the site, completely blocking it from public view. Street closures were necessary, and traffic began backing up as police officers ordered drivers to turn in every direction except the one they desired.

"Temporary alteration of traffic patterns is to be expected, and commuters should anticipate delays west of Howard Street," wrote Dylan. "But the improvement to the city will be well worth a few small detours. The mayor has pointed out that those who live and work downtown will now have a greater incentive than ever to use our excellent public transportation system. Urban planning experts have praised the comprehensive attention to detail and public convenience in the staging of this project."

Within an hour, he completed his assignment and picked up his desk phone to call Captain Bollard. Her phone rang three times and switched over to phone mail. He left a message, then stood up and decided to have a look out in the hallway; but when he tried the door, he found that he was locked in.

As he stood by the door scratching his head, his cell phone rang. It was Sidney.

"It's happened," sobbed Sidney. Her voice was garbled by poor signal. "They've suspended me for the rest of the year!"

"Suspended you! Are you going to get paid?" asked Dylan.

"I don't know. The letter didn't say. It just said, 'You have been found guilty of discrimination and are herewith suspended as of this date. You may not return to campus without written permission from the Dean. Failure to abide by the terms of suspension will result in legal action including but not limited to fines and/or imprisonment.'"

Dylan could not hear every word, but he caught enough to understand that she could not return to work. "*I will call Armand.*" He spoke loudly and slowly, hoping that she would be able to hear him. "*He said that he could help.* Hello. Hello." He had lost the call. When he tried to call back, the phone registered "no service." He tried standing in different parts of the room, with no better success. Then the desk phone rang. To his relief, Armand was calling.

"How's your article coming?" inquired Black. There was loud machinery in the background.

"I'm done, but I'm locked in the office!" shouted Dylan.

"Good, good!" Black shouted back.

Dylan concluded that he had not made himself heard. "I said I'm locked in! And I can't get through to Captain Bollard. But listen, listen: Sidney just got suspended—basically fired! Can you pull some strings for us?"

"Sidney's fired? Oh. Bad news, old chap! *(No, no, over there. To the left! Watch that stone!)* Sorry, I'm at the work site downtown. No use trying to talk now. I'll see what we can do. Later."

There was a dial tone. Dylan sat down and re-read his article. It had practically written itself, he thought. He checked the time on the computer screen: 11:00. The list of points to be covered included instructions on where to send his finished work. He sent it off. A second call to Bollard's office went immediately to voice mail. He left a second message. His cell phone still showed no service.

At 12:30, the door opened suddenly, and Livvy Bollard loomed in the doorframe. She was carrying a folder. "Are you done yet?" she demanded, as if she thought he'd been slacking. Not waiting for an answer, she closed the door behind her, and in three strides, crowded in next to Dylan, facing the computer. A club hanging at her left hip smacked against his right ear, and he pulled away.

"I finished it," he answered sullenly, "Now what?"

"There's a rather urgent article you need to do next. It has to do with your landlord, Dr. Evan Fitzgerald. Did you know he's a neo-Nazi? You ought to be more careful what company you keep; know what I'm saying?"

Dylan sat with his mouth open. "Nah, no way," he said after a pause.

Livvy Bollard slapped her folder on the desk, spun round and slammed him back against the wall. She stood straddling his knees, gripping his chin with her left hand. Her red-polished fingernails dug into his cheeks as she brought her face down to the level of his own. "You didn't just contradict me, did you, sweetie?" she whispered.

Dylan's eyes were wide. "No, no, I was just…"

She knocked the back of his head against the wall again. "What?"

"Not contradicting, no," he stammered.

She smiled. "Good." Letting him go as abruptly as she had seized him, she stood up straight, still straddling him and pinning his swivel chair to the wall. "The folder on the desk contains all the facts and verbiage you need to write the article. Fitzgerald is scheduled to give a lecture this evening at the old folks' home around the corner from his house. It will be a violent, white-supremacist, racist, Nazi rant. Persons offended by his hateful speech will stage a protest. Fitzgerald will be taken into custody by the police. Got it?"

Dylan sat in stunned silence.

Bollard tilted her head to the side, leaned forward a little, and shouted, "*Got it?*"

Dylan jumped involuntarily. He nodded. The chief of security nodded in reply and left the room. The door slammed behind her.

For several minutes, he sat staring at the door in disbelief. His head ached, but he was not sure whether that was Captain Bollard's doing or a consequence of missing lunch.

The folder lay in front of him. He opened it. There was a list of bullet points:

> *Dr. Evan Fitzgerald (EF) is associated with known far-right, racist, white-suprema-*

cist, nativist, hate groups. (Use all these terms in the article.)

EF delivered a foam-flecked, hateful speech to an all-white audience at Roland Park Place, at 7 pm Thursday, denouncing the removal of Confederate monuments in Baltimore. (Use the words "spewed" and "lashed out." Say that he started with "racist dogwhistles," and when the audience cheered, he went on to overtly racist rhetoric.)

Describe some members of the audience walking out in disgust.

EF made anti-Semitic statements including denouncing the Holocaust Memorial (use your imagination here).

note: We have sent a report to the Southern Poverty Law Center. Just go to their website and search EF's name. Be sure to quote the SPLC as a "reliable source."

Anti-fascist activists staged a non-violent protest but were shut down by police.

EF shouted abuse at the demonstrators and the police before being "taken into custody." (Be sure not to say "arrested.")

Have article ready to publish by 5 pm.

Dylan ran a hand through his hair. How was this possible? They were demanding that he put his name to a report on an event that had not happened yet. He had grown accustomed to learning that seemingly respectable people, even very famous people, could suddenly turn out to be vile racists, "literally Hitler," or sexual predators. He remembered the words of his favorite comic-book hero, *The Shadow*: "Who knows what evil lurks in the hearts of men? The Shadow knows!" But even the Shadow's powers did not extend to writing the news ahead of time.

"Maybe," he said to himself, "the story is *basically* true without being entirely *factual*. Fitzgerald has backward opinions, and he even tried to impose his views on *me* the other night. He had no right to do that. Yeah. That's kind of fascistic, trying to tell me what to do!"

He puffed out his chest as he thought of giving the arrogant geezer his comeuppance. Then he thought of his argument with Sidney about the Fitzgeralds. Those people had even turned his own wife against him! "Wait until Sidney reads this!" he muttered as he began to type.

After about an hour, he had a rough draft. He believed that he had become fairly adept at stitching together snippets of information to create a fluent story, but this effort had proved to be surprisingly taxing. His newspaper work had trained him to check the reliability of his sources. Even if that diligence extended only as far as making sure that the names were spelled correctly and the direct quotes were "close enough," he had still acquired a mental discipline that did not support outright confabulation. This assignment was as if he had been handed a map that directed him to drive his car across a ditch and into a plowed field.

Dylan stood up and stretched. His bladder ached. He had not been to the bathroom since leaving home, and he saw that it was past two in the afternoon. Now that the urge had become acute, he could think of nothing else. He tried the door. Useless. The only inside line he knew was Bollard's, and he had no desire to call that! The room was bare except for the desk, the chair, a wire wastebasket, a poster on the wall showing all sorts of people holding hands under a huge, computer-generated rainbow, with the legend: "GOOD, Moving Forward Together." And there was a spindly, dismal-looking ficus tree in a large pot in one corner. It looked as if it could use watering. Would anyone notice if he watered it? Maybe not.

Relieved for the moment, Dylan returned to the computer. His earlier anger at Dr. Fitzgerald had cooled. He remembered an occasion when, at the age of sixteen, he had written an insulting note to a friend over some trifling disagreement. He had written the letter on Saturday, knowing that he wouldn't be able to mail it until Monday. By the time he managed to find and address an envelope on Sunday afternoon, he reread the letter, regretted the words he had used, and tore it all to pieces. He also recalled other spiteful letters, ones that had hit their intended targets, and that he dearly wished he could have called back.

Then he thought of Sidney and the look she would have on her face when she learned that he, her own husband, had smeared the good name of someone she admired. His eyes skimmed the document, and his hand drifted to the computer mouse. One moment, the words were highlighted in blue; the next moment, the page was blank.

Dylan sighed deeply. Now what? His headache had returned, and he was hungry. The desk had seven drawers, three on each side and one in the middle. The center drawer contained only dust and a few mouse droppings. The left drawers were locked. In the top right drawer was a bent paper clip, more dust, more mouse droppings, and an opened package of saltines, with one cracker missing. He placed the package on the top of the desk and regarded it critically. It did not appear to have been chewed. One tentative bite, then another, and the crackers were on their way through his stomach.

The lower two drawers on the right remained unexplored. The second one was empty. The bottom drawer contained a chewed packet of mouse poison. Dylan noticed that his mouth was dry. What if the crackers had poison in them?

Or some kind of mouse germs? No use thinking that way. He got up and tried to distract himself by running in place. Then he tried his cell phone again. Still no service. Maybe he could call Sidney from the desk phone. No outside line. Internet? The message "ACCESS FORBIDDEN" appeared across the screen.

By five o'clock, he was slumped at the desk. The sound of the door latch startled him awake. The pimply, bespectacled face of GOOD's data analyst Justin Goldberg peered around the door. "Writer's block?" he asked as he squeezed in and closed the door as if to prevent the escape of a cat or dog. In his left hand was a chilled bottle of water. He opened it and took a swig.

"The Chair is not going to be happy," he continued. "Only your second assignment, and you're past the deadline with nothing to show." He reached in front of Dylan and touched the space bar. The screen lit up. Two mouse clicks, and the entire text of Dylan's fabricated hit piece reappeared. "Well, what do you know! You did write it. It needs polishing, but there it is. So why did you delete it?"

Dylan swallowed hard. He was thirsty and hungry. His head ached. "It's not right," he choked.

"I don't think you understand. If you work for us, *you* don't get to decide what is right. You are part of a worldwide struggle. Your personal opinion doesn't count. Besides, things could go even worse for your buddy Fitzgerald. We could change the script. He could be charged with something and actually arrested. Illegal drugs could be found in his house. A female patient could make an allegation of sexual assault. Or maybe something happens to you. Did you open the email I sent you? Yes? Maybe now you already have child porn on your home computer. Do you know how long you can be put away for that? Or Sidney. Something really embarrassing and awful could happen to her, you know what I mean? So, get back to work."

Dylan was too shaken to react before Justin slipped out and closed the door, taking his bottle of water with him.

Dr. Fitzgerald walked briskly. Fast walking was a lifelong habit, and he had come to believe that it also conferred some survival value in Baltimore City. Tucked under his arm was a box containing a slide carousel. His destination was just around the corner from his own house. Roland Park Place was an up-scale retirement community in a smart-looking, modern brick high-rise on West 40th Street. It was also the home of one of Fitzgerald's patients, who had invited his doc to give a presentation for the regular Thursday evening lecture series. The topic of the lecture was "The Monumental City." It was a talk that he had given many times over the years, but the title had acquired an ironic twist since so many monuments had been "disappeared" of late.

Ten minutes before seven, the auditorium was already full. Old people who favor the structured life of a retirement home tend to be very punctual. There was a brief introduction by Mrs. Todd, the events coordinator. The house lights dimmed, and the projector came on.

"Thank you, Mrs. Todd, ladies and gentlemen. I appreciate both your invitation to speak and your willingness to accommodate my antiquated visual aids." The doctor looked out at his audience and smiled, hoping that the projector bulb would last out the evening. A new one might be hard to find. The screen showed the title of the talk.

"Most of you, I know, are from around here; so you are familiar with some of Baltimore's traditions, such as *(click)* colorful political figures" (picture of Mayor William Donald Schaefer at the opening of the seal pool at the National Aquarium, dressed in an old-style striped two-piece bathing suit and carrying a yellow rubber ducky), *(click)* "optimistic, if counterfactual, messages on bus-stop benches" (photo of someone sleeping under a newspaper on a bench; the back of the bench bears the stenciled motto: Baltimore, The City That Reads/ Kurt L. Schmoke, Mayor), *(click)* "parades in honor of our heroic past. This is the bicentennial Defenders Day Parade, celebrating the repulse of the British on September the 14th, 1814. We can take pride in the curious fact that more Baltimore patriots have died celebrating the Battle of Baltimore than died fighting it." *(click)*

"And, of course, monuments. Baltimore has been called the Monumental City. (It's been called other things, of course, with equal validity, but we'll leave those for another day.) Here you see a lithograph of America's first monument to George Washington, completed in 1829. If you came from out-of-town and had no time for anything else, the parks around Mount Vernon Square would be a good choice, with one of the richest assortments of monuments and architectural treasures in the whole city."

He continued in this vein for about half an hour, avoiding controversial topics but emphasizing the esthetic and educational value of the city's statuary.

Suddenly, the doors in the back of the room burst open, and a scruffy rabble filed in. There were about a dozen of them, and they wore T-shirts and blue jeans. Some had on hoodies that partly hid their faces. Four of them carried signs: "Down With White Supremacy," "End Racism," "Silence The Fascist Pigs," and "Nazis Deserve To Die." They immediately began chanting and jeering. Thirty-two elderly heads turned around to see what all the ruckus was.

Dr. Fitzgerald leaned into the microphone and shouted, "I think you've come to the wrong meeting!" A codger in a pale blue suit opened his eyes and stood up suddenly. His hearing aids were switched to the public-address system, and he had been dozing pleasantly until this moment. Seeing the mob in the back of the auditorium, he grabbed his chest and exclaimed, "Oh! Oh! What are they?" His wife helped him to a nitroglycerin tablet as the chanting grew louder and the hecklers advanced on the podium.

Just in time, as it seemed, six green-uniformed police rushed in behind the agitators. Two of them forced their way to the front, grabbed Dr. Fitzgerald by the arms, and pushed him toward the emergency exit. A third picked up the microphone and announced, "This meeting is over. Please clear the room. I repeat, this meeting is over. In the interest of safety, please clear the room." The other two officers held their arms outstretched to keep the protesters at bay. As he found himself being shoved into the back of an unmarked car with flashing red-and-blue lights, the erstwhile lecturer saw that other protesters were jumping around in the middle of 40th Street and blocking traffic.

In another unmarked car, *without* flashing lights, idling in the no-parking zone in front of a liquor store on Roland Avenue, Livvy Bollard watched the action on two small TV screens. A vein in her forehead was standing out, and her face was crimson. "Botched!" she screamed. "Botched!" She turned to her driver. "With these operations, you *never,*

NEVER let the target speak! How are we supposed to control the narrative if you let him speak?"

"But, but they started early! And the Antifa bus got stuck in traffic!"

"I want results, not excuses! And make sure you grab his slides!" The chief of the GOOD police flounced out of the car and slammed the door. As the car sped off, she walked up the street to the Fitzgeralds' house.

The front door was already open, and she stomped into the Fitzgeralds' apartment. Looking down the long hall, she saw a uniformed officer of the city police standing outside the door of the back bedroom. Well, at least this part of the operation was going smoothly. Her instructions had been, "Round up the Mrs. and the dogs and anybody else you find; and keep them in the back of the house while we execute our warrant."

"You searched the back bedroom before you shut them in it?" she called to the cop on guard.

"Nothing there," he replied, "And we pulled everything apart."

"All right," she said, her anger dissipating as she pulled out the piece of paper she had received from the professor. She held it up to the city cop. "Nothing that looked like this?"

He glanced at it and shook his head.

It took a couple of hours, but she enjoyed every minute. She loved tearing through other people's stuff. It gave her almost as intense an erotic charge as a good interrogation. She emptied every drawer and tore apart every file of historic papers, but the letter in question was simply not there. She kicked over a ceramic umbrella stand and was pleased by the way it cracked in two. Oh, well, if she couldn't get it out of the house, she'd get it out of the owner. But there was still the second floor!

Baltimore has many empty warehouses, and it was one of these that Captain Bollard had chosen as a "dark site," where she could lock up troublemakers outside of the regular jail system. The building was of red brick and occupied about half a block. The rest of the block consisted of boarded-up row houses. Weeds, trash, and graffiti completed the exterior décor. The only outward evidences of occupancy were a pair of new overhead doors, outdoor cameras, and security lighting.

The inside was no less dismal, but it showed more modifications. A row of dimly-lit prison cells had been constructed in the back, eight-foot cubes of concrete block. The floors and walls were damp, and there was a pervasive odor of oil, a reminder of the days when the building housed a machine shop. The main bay was cavernous, with a twenty-foot ceiling. A clank and a grinding noise announced the opening of one of the big doors, and a black Ford Taurus slid inside. The darkly-tinted windows completely concealed its occupants.

When the overhead door had completed its descent, the back doors of the car opened, and two green-uniformed officers emerged, motioning for their passenger to climb out as well. Dr. Fitzgerald straightened his back and appraised his surroundings.

"What is this?" he asked. "What's going on?"

"You've been taken into custody," replied the shorter of the two cops.

"You have no right to arrest me," protested Fitzgerald, taking a step toward a door in the outer wall.

The taller cop seized his arm. "I wouldn't try that," he growled. "And you're not under arrest. You're in protective custody. The protesters who disrupted your lecture made a death threat. We can't release you until our investigative unit has been able to ascertain that you are no longer at risk. Step this way."

By now, the driver had joined the other two policemen, who pushed the doctor into one of the cells and closed the door. It was a solid steel door with a tiny window. Fitzgerald tried the handle. Locked. He looked around. The cell contained a low cot with a bare mattress, a metal straight chair, a sink, and a toilet. The only light came from a bare bulb in the ceiling. Seeing no way out, he sat down to wait.

Sidney had finished out her day of teaching. Her immediate supervisor, Judy Armacost, had not received any notice of suspension, and she declined to do anything without a direct order from a higher level of the county bureaucracy. "This kind of thing happens more often than you'd think, and it's unwise to overreact." she commented.

"I suppose it would be trite to say that I feel as if I'm in a play by Kafka," remarked Sidney with a nervous laugh.

"Mm, yes, yes, perhaps it would," replied Judy, who had gone back to shuffling papers.

So it was that Sidney returned to the apartment at six in the evening. Dylan had not texted to inform her of his plans. "If he can't let me know what he's doing, I'll go ahead without him," she thought. In the refrigerator, she found shrimp salad, a tomato, and an avocado. Just the meal for a warm spring evening. But first, a glass of Chardonnay and a bath, with her favorite scented bath salts. She had read that the salt soaks out all kinds of toxins, and even "bad energy." That was the treatment she needed.

After a good long soak, she dried herself with a clean towel and put on her satin bathrobe. Throwing open the French doors at the back of the bedroom, she decided that this was a perfect time to wash her underwear by hand and hang them out to dry on the back balcony. Washing intimate apparel in a shared machine in the basement had bothered her all along. Now that the weather was nice, she was ready with a brand-new clothes line. She removed the plastic wrapper and tied one end of the line to the post at the southwest corner of the covered balcony and stretched the cord across to a cleat on the northeast corner. The excess cord she coiled in the corner. She had also bought fresh, new clothes pins, not like the old, darkened ones in the basement.

When she had washed and hung the garments, she admired her work. The clothesline added a cheerful, domestic touch. Her white cotton blouse hung over a chair. Tomorrow there would be time to take it to the dry cleaner on the corner. She hummed a little tune as she walked barefoot to the kitchen.

Her pleasant reverie was broken by a loud pounding at the door. Her heart began racing. What could be the matter? Hastily opening the door, she saw a tall woman in a green uniform, with a look in her eye that produced an instinctive response in Sidney. She slammed the door shut. But the police woman had placed her shiny black boot in the way. Faster than she could react, Sidney felt herself driven backward, spun around, and handcuffed.

"I am Captain Bollard, and I am here to execute a warrant to search these premises for evidence in connection with an incidence of hate speech and incitement to riot." As she spoke, she propelled Sidney down the hall to the bedroom.

"You can't treat me like this. I have rights!" shouted Sidney, struggling to free her arm from Bollard's bruising grasp.

"You'll be lucky if I don't arrest you for interfering with a police officer," snarled the captain, pushing her hard against one of the posts of the bed and untying the sash of her robe. In a quick motion, Bollard pulled the ends of the sash back around the bedpost and tied them together. The robe fell open. Sidney's wrists were fastened behind her back by the handcuffs, and now her arms were tied to the bed by her bathrobe sash. She began to scream. Bollard snatched the thin cotton blouse off the chair and gagged her with it, tying the arms of the blouse to the bedpost. Then she took out her truncheon and slid it slowly up and down the front of her captive.

"Now, are you going to stay very still while I conduct my search?" asked the cop. Sidney nodded, wide-eyed.

Bollard replaced the truncheon in her belt and produced a flashlight, which she shone behind all the larger pieces of furniture and into the recesses of all the closets. She opened electrical panels and took the covers off the radiators. After a half-hour search, she returned to the bedroom. Sidney had managed to untie the sash and had tried to slip out of the gag; but it had slid downward, around her neck, and she was unable to reach up to free it.

"Disobeying a lawful order, I see," said Bollard. "Attempting to harm yourself while in police custody. Apparently, more restraint is in order." Her gaze fell upon the clothesline, where Sidney's bra and panties hung, dark against the fading pink of the western sky. In an instant, the captain was on the balcony, cutting loose the coil of extra cord and carrying it back into the bedroom.

"This should hold you," she said, tossing the rope onto the bed and untying the gag from the bedpost. Just as she was forcing Sidney backward, a voice called down the hall, "Captain Bollard! Captain Bollard! There's a lawyer here!"

"Damn!" said the captain. She turned Sidney toward the bed and bent her over the mattress. Leaning close to her ear, she whispered as she unlocked the handcuffs, "My search is completed. You are at liberty to move about your apartment. And pull yourself together."

As soon as her tormenter was gone, Sidney ran to the door and locked it. Would the policewoman try to come back? There were no weapons at hand, except a large kitchen knife, which she retrieved from a drawer. The evening had turned cool, and she found herself shivering. Grasping the knife tightly, she went in search of some warm clothes.

After Justin's rapid departure, Dylan ran to the door. To open so easily, it must have been unlocked the whole time that Justin was in the room. He tried the knob. It turned. But did he dare open the door? Would Captain Bollard be standing in the corridor? Would the leaders of GOOD, with its vast resources, crush him like a bug if he defied them?

Dylan returned to the desk and stared at the computer screen, paralyzed by indecision. He remembered Armand Black's remarks about Sir Thomas More sacrificing himself for nothing. And he remembered the Chair's words, "I require neither more nor less than absolute loyalty and obedience."

"Let's think this through logically," Dylan told himself. But logic did not come easily to him. He frowned. These people were demanding that he sign off on a story that they made up in advance of anything actually happening. So, they were essentially ordering him to lie, to violate his own principles as some kind of loyalty test. It was like an initiation.

He paced back and forth. "If I make myself a party to this lie," he said in a low voice, "I may hurt Dr. Fitzgerald, but I may prevent them from doing something even worse to him, or his wife, or me, or my wife." He paced some more. "But they could do any or all of those other things anyway. And if they did, that would be their responsibility, not mine. I can take responsibility only for what I do, and I have a duty to follow my ethical standards."

With the sensation of jumping into an abyss, he deleted the article again; but he knew that no matter how he tried to erase it, Justin would be able to call it back. So, he unplugged the computer. It was one of those all-in-one-piece desktop models with a separate keyboard. He disconnected all the wires, lifted the computer above his head, and dashed it repeatedly against the corner of the desk, stopping only when a shard of plastic gouged his hand.

Now to get out of here! Taking a deep breath, he gripped the doorknob. This time, it did not turn.

Livvy Bollard was in a foul mood when she arrived at the grim warehouse near 25th Street. She had spent the afternoon arguing with a Baltimore City judge, who was supposed to be bought-and-paid-for, to get a simple search warrant. She had even dragged Mr. Wheedler with her as legal backup. But the judge had been skeptical, and she had found it necessary to produce a couple of forged affidavits that she had brought along as a last resort. Even then, the judge had insisted on Baltimore City cops being present. If her own people had had the place to themselves, things would have been very different. And then Mrs. Fitzgerald had called her lawyer after being shut up in the back bedroom! And *he* had arrived at a particularly inconvenient moment.

Dr. Fitzgerald could hear the big door of the warehouse grinding open and closed, and he smelled the exhaust of Captain Bollard's car. The cell door opened, and Bollard stalked in with two other muscular women in green uniforms.

"Cuff him to the chair," she ordered. Standing in front of her prisoner, she unfolded her copy of the note from John Reuben Thompson to Dr. Evan Fitzgerald, Senior.

"Have you ever seen this letter?" she asked, without preamble.

"I can't read it without my glasses," replied the doctor, who could actually see it well enough to identify it as a rough draft of the one that he had so recently taken pains to conceal.

"Then I'll read it to you," snarled Bollard. After struggling through the first couple of paragraphs, she leaned close and asked, "Well?"

"I have never seen that letter, until now, that is," he answered. "How did you get it? Was it *purloined*?"

"Was it *what*?"

Dr. Fitzgerald concluded that he was *not* dealing with a Poe scholar. "Was it *stolen*?" he asked.

"*I'll* ask the questions here," shouted Bollard. "And I don't believe you've never seen this letter before!"

Dr. Fitzgerald shrugged. "Believe what you like," he said.

Livvy Bollard narrowed her eyes. "I believe you're going to tell me exactly what I want to know." She slapped him across the face. "That's just for starters, doc. Do you know, back at your house, I've got your wife in custody? She's, what, almost seventy years old? It's so easy for bad stuff to happen with folks that age, you know? Head injuries, broken bones, suffocation, all kinds of risks that you'd probably want to avoid by cooperating with us."

This sort of threat was exactly what Fitzgerald had been expecting. "You *wouldn't!*" he gasped in mock terror.

"In a heartbeat, buddy, in a heartbeat," replied Bollard with a triumphant smile.

"*If* I had the letter, and *if* I gave it to you, would you go away and leave us in peace?" he asked.

"Scout's honor," said Livvy Bollard.

Fitzgerald gave her a skeptical look. "I can't do anything about it until tomorrow."

"Why not?"

"I have to get into my safe-deposit box," he replied. "Take me home, and I'll see that you get it tomorrow."

"Oh, no you don't. I'm keeping you where I can see you until you give me that letter!"

The city cops, whose names and badge numbers Paul wrote down in a notebook, mumbled their apologies for the "inconvenience" they had caused and drove away in their squad car. Rose Fitzgerald's phone rang. "Are they all gone, *all* of them?" asked Sidney's voice.

"Yes, dear, they're all gone, but I don't like this. I don't feel safe staying here," said Rose.

"You aren't going to leave me here alone?" cried Sidney.

"Of course not, dear, but there may not be much time. Pack a few things. We may have to stay away for a few days."

In less than ten minutes, Rose and Sidney were climbing into Paul Anderssen's big four-wheel-drive pickup. The dogs panted excitedly, happy for a road trip. Paul drove a circuitous course, along winding farm roads, to be sure that they were not followed. Ninety minutes later, they arrived safely at Wanda's farmhouse.

Chapter 14

At 8 am, the black Ford Taurus carrying Dr. Fitzgerald and Captain Bollard drew up in front of the Fitzgeralds' house. The driver kept the engine idling while the policewoman followed the doctor inside. Taped to the front door of his apartment, he found a note from Rose: *Two chickens in the fridge. Expect you for dinner with company.* The pre-arranged message meant that both of the women in the house were at Wanda's farm, and that he was to rejoin the company there.

Walking slowly into his study, he shook his head at the mess that Bollard had made. The drawers of his roll-top desk were scattered over the floor. From one small drawer, he removed a safe-deposit key.

The Roland Park branch of M&T Bank opened at half past eight, and Bollard was standing beside Dr. Fitzgerald at the front door when the manager unlocked it. She waited impatiently while he entered the vault with the manager and carried the long, metal box into a small private stall. There, he opened the box and removed a gun, his father's service pistol, a Colt Model 1911 with a dull, blue-gray finish. Once he gave this rent-a-cop what she wanted, she might decide that he was expendable. Tucking the pistol in the back of his waistband, he next removed a small antique key. After returning the box to the vault, he walked out, holding up the key as he passed the frowning Bollard.

Back in his study one more, he held up the small key and glanced about him vaguely. He scratched his head. "Oh! Now I remember!" he said. "I didn't need this after all. Memory isn't what it used to be. The letter isn't in the compartment that this key opens."

Bollard glared at him menacingly.

"Yes, yes, it's over here!" he announced, picking up the resealed envelope from the AMA and tearing it open. "I don't know why I forgot!" And he handed her a fragile, yellowed envelope bearing a three-cent stamp.

Bollard snatched it from his hand and opened it. Inside was the letter with the coded message that she had been instructed to find. "I don't know what your little game was, buddy, wasting my time at the bank. You're just lucky this is what I was after! And if you know what's good for you, you won't be running your mouth about *any* of this, to *anyone*!"

Dr. Fitzgerald took a step back from her with his hand on his right hip. The pistol in the back of his waistband was hidden by his tweed jacket. The hammer was down, with a round in the chamber. He glared at her. To his relief, the captain turned on her heel and left. He locked the doors as soon as she had hurried back to her car.

Once behind the tinted glass of the Taurus, Livvy Bollard carefully placed the letter in a clear zip-lock bag, then took out her cell phone and called headquarters to report her triumph. "And turn loose that retard, Joe what's-his-name," she added. "We don't need him anymore, but with that chip in his neck, he might just lead us to whoever sent him to check out Poe's grave."

Evan Fitzgerald spent the rest of the morning tidying his house. After a light lunch, he drove to his office, one of several similar small medical offices in a drab, two-story building on Falls Road near Coldspring Lane. There were two patients scheduled for that afternoon. The first was an asthmatic who worried about herself and came for frequent checkups, and the second was a former steam-fitter at Sparrows Point, who returned episodically for management of his high blood pressure and chronic lung disease. He was a long talker, and Dr. Fitzgerald enjoyed his tales of the glory days of the shipyards and steel mill.

Just as he was about to lock up and leave, Fitzpatrick saw a man in a winter coat loping towards him. He noted that the

fellow had the gait and facial expression of a mental defec-
tive. Not unusual in the vicinity of Hampden. Then he recognized him.

"Joe!" he called out, "Joe, what's happened to you? Come inside!" He ushered him in, while glancing back for signs of pursuit.

Joe, always literal-minded, launched into a highly detailed account of everything that had happened to him
since January, when he had brought a rose and a bottle of
cognac to Poe's grave. As he talked, he scratched at the
back of his neck.

"Let me have a look at that," said the doctor, putting
on his glasses. "This cut is getting infected. And what's
this? I feel a foreign object. Did they implant something
in your neck?"

"I dunno. They put me on a cold table and poked me back
there. With a needle, I think."

"Wait a second," said the doctor, rummaging in a drawer.
This will feel cold." He swabbed the spot with antiseptic and
popped open an ampule of lidocaine, the contents of which
he drew up through a needle into a syringe. Discarding the
first needle, he attached a new 25-gauge needle, saying,
"Now a little pinch. A little burning," and he injected the lidocaine around the cut. As he pushed the needle deeper, he
could feel it clicking against the embedded chip. "Let's give
that numbing medicine some time to work."

On a stainless-steel tray, he laid a sterile drape, onto which he dropped a disposable scalpel, a slender stainless clamp, and a stack of gauze sponges. With the scalpel, he widened the cut in the skin. Probing with the clamp, he found that its jaws were still too restricted by the small opening. "Bear with me here," he said as he made the cut wider. It began to bleed, and he compressed it with a gauze pad while reintroducing the clamp. This time he was able to grab the chip, but when he pulled, the clamp slipped off. After several tries, pushing down with his left hand and pulling with his right, he succeeded in removing the foreign object.

"Well, what do you know!" he exclaimed. He held in his hand a silvery lozenge, the size and shape of a vitamin capsule. "We got it out, Joe. Good job. I doubt they would have put more than one tracking device in you, but let's give you a quick once-over, shall we? First I'll put a bandage on you."

After applying some gauze and tape, he opened a desk drawer. There he found the chewing gum that he had confiscated from his last receptionist, who had persisted in chewing in front of patients. He unwrapped two pieces of gum and popped them into his mouth.

Finding no other suspicious devices on Joe or in his clothing, he hurried Joe outside and had him sit in his car while he walked to the bus stop on Coldspring Lane, where a lumbering, boxy vehicle was discharging passengers. Fitzgerald mounted the front step. "Is this the bus for the Inner Harbor?" he called to the driver.

"No, you wants the 28, goin' the other way. Or either you just takes the light rail."

"Thanks," shouted Fitzgerald, patting the doorframe as he jumped down. The doors closed with a hiss, and the bus lurched and wallowed away. As it did so, the wad of gum containing the chip began a long tour of the city.

It was four in the afternoon when Linda came running into the farm house. "Evan is here, and he's brought Joe! He's found Joe!"

Wanda and her husband Paul hurried to the door just in time to greet the missing person and the detainee. "Were you followed?" asked Paul, who had retrieved a rifle from the hall closet.

"I took all precautions," replied Evan Fitzgerald, "so I think not. They may believe that they got what they wanted anyway. You were right about the letter, Wanda. They were actually after a piece of blue paper that was enclosed with it, not the letter itself. It seems they already had a complete copy. I presume Thompson saved the rough draft and then wrote what they used to call a 'fair copy' to my ancestor. What they really wanted to find, I destroyed."

Rose Fitzgerald appeared at the door with Sidney. "Oh, Evan, thank God!" she cried, throwing her arms around her husband, who returned her embrace. Sidney held out her hand to him, and he squeezed it.

"And Joe!" exclaimed Wanda. "For a while, we were afraid we might have lost you forever. What happened to you?"

"I got on the train at Hunt Valley, and it was cold outside, but the inside of the train was warmer. The train had only two cars, and one was empty, and there was a guy in the other wearing a green, shiny coat, kinda puffy, you know, with a hood."

"Joe," interrupted the doctor, "Perhaps if you don't mind, I'll just give an executive summary of what you told me on the way here."

Joe shrugged.

"Come, come," said Wanda, "you both look tired. Let's all sit in the living room, and Paul will bring in some sherry."

When they had settled themselves, Dr. Fitzgerald resumed, "Apparently someone attacked Joe at the graveyard and hit him in the head. He didn't see the assailant, but when he regained consciousness, he was in a cell inside a warehouse, which sounds like the same place they took me. A big woman in a green uniform beat him repeatedly and subjected him to some tortures that I forbear to discuss with ladies present. She kept asking him who sent him, where he came from, what he was after, what he knew. They deprived him of sleep, food, and water until he was delirious, but through it all, he kept silent. Then they transported him to what sounds like a mental asylum and drugged him into a stupor. He doesn't remember much more until they, as he says, 'poked the back of his neck,' implanting a chip. That was just a couple of days ago. After they extorted the letter from me, they released him, evidently with the idea of following him here."

Paul bounded out of his chair. "And you brought him!"

Dr. Fitzgerald raised a hand. "It's all right. I removed the chip and attached it to a Baltimore City bus. May it lead them a merry chase."

"But wait a minute," objected Paul. "You said they think they got what they wanted, but that you destroyed the paper that was enclosed with the letter. Wasn't that what they wanted? I don't understand."

Fitzgerald smiled. "Sorry I wasn't clear," he replied. He drew a pen and a pad of note paper from a pocket of his jacket. On the paper, he wrote the following numbers:

12 124

112 121 21 18 24

56 57

28 45 23 43 32

"John Reuben Thompson was a literary man, but unlike Poe, he had no interest in codes and ciphers. I examined the cipher years ago, thinking that it was probably keyed to another document. The obvious candidate was the poem 'Annabel Lee,' which Poe had rolled up around it. Not to bore you with all the possibilities, suffice to say that I found that if you take the first digit of each number as identifying a line of the poem, and the next digit or digits as a letter, the message reads, 'To drink is death.' Now, I have no idea what Poe meant by that. The most sensible interpretation was that he was merely asserting that if he broke his pledge of abstinence, he would die. Poe had no way of anticipating that the message would accompany a letter referring to 'materials,' possibly potions, that someone could drink. But his mind was on both matters when he handed Thompson the manuscript, so who knows?"

"You still haven't explained why our adversaries think they got what they wanted," said Wanda.

"The slip of paper was twice as large as it needed to be. The lower half was blank," replied Fitzgerald, "so I cut the paper in half and recopied the first three lines onto the blank sheet, changing the fourth line and adding a fifth, a simple matter if you know the poem. Then I burned the original."

"And you changed to message to what?" asked Paul.

"The revised message reads 'To drink is to live.' I decided to give those people the opposite of whatever it was they intended to learn."

"And what if the blank sheet that you gave them with the revised message *wasn't really blank*?" asked Paul. "Didn't Poe experiment with invisible ink?"

Fitzgerald had been rather satisfied with himself until this moment. "I never thought of that," he gasped.

Meanwhile, Captain Bollard and Armand Black were standing in the Chair's office, examining a piece of blue paper. It was still in the clear plastic bag. "Well," demanded Pyknos, "what does it mean?"

Black scratched his chin in his best professorial manner. "The paper appears to be of the correct type for the period. As for the pencil, there's no way to date that. It's just graphite and kaolin." He opened the plastic bag and extracted the paper with tweezers. There was a gooseneck lamp on the desk, and Black straightened its neck and switched it on. Holding the paper very close to the light bulb, he pulled a magnifying glass from his left coat pocket.

Pyknos swiveled his wheelchair impatiently. "Now what?" he asked.

"I'm checking for a watermark. Unlikely to find one, but… what's this?" Letters were appearing as the bulb heated the paper. They spelled out, "EUREKA." The word appeared at the top of the paper, and the first line of numbers very slightly overlapped it.

"Mr. Pyknos, I believe that this coded message relates to Poe's secret discovery," announced the professor, holding up the paper. "Now to decipher it!"

"Get Justin up here!" Pyknos shouted into the intercom. Turning to Bollard and Black, he said, "That will be all. We need a real brain on this!"

An hour later, Justin had discovered the answer. The chair looked at the decoded words. It was as he had foreseen. "To drink is to live."

At Wanda's farm house, the friends continued to recount their experiences over the last few days. Sidney shared her fears of losing her job and her anxiety about Dylan's whereabouts, which concerned her all the more after hearing of GOOD's abduction of Joe and Dr. Fitzgerald.

"I am confident that your husband is safe, said Wanda. "Yes, they are telling me that he will not come to harm; but he is passing through a trial." Her eyes were closed, and she sat with her palms turned upward. "More than that I cannot tell."

"Well, I can tell you this, young lady," said Paul, who had returned from the kitchen. "What you went through is not unusual these days, and people have been persecuted as you were, by what I call black racists, for the last twenty years at least. I still have some connections with the small sane remnant of the county government, and I believe we can make this stupid business go away. But what I came to say is, dinner is served!"

When all had filed into the dining room and taken their seats, and when all the plates were filled, Wanda bowed her head and said, "Thank you, gracious Father, for returning our loved ones to us, and for supplying this food for our sustenance. Amen." Turning to Dr. Fitzgerald, she said, "Evan, these are days of peril. Would you be kind enough to say another prayer, for our country?"

"Of course.

> *"Almighty God, we make our earnest prayer that Thou wilt keep the United States in Thy holy protection, that Thou wilt incline the hearts of the citizens to cultivate a spirit of subordination and obedience to government; and entertain a brotherly affection and love for one another and for their fellow citizens of the United States of America at large, And finally that Thou wilt most graciously be pleased to dispose us all to do justice, to love mercy, and to demean ourselves with that*

charity, humility and pacific temper of mind
which were the characteristics of The Divine
Author of our blessed religion, and without
whose example in these things we can never
hope to be a happy nation. Grant our suppli-
cation, we beseech Thee, through Jesus Christ
Our Lord. Amen."

"That's lovely," said Sidney. "Where did that prayer come from?"

"From the first days of our republic," answered Dr. Fitzgerald. "George Washington himself composed it, and he sent it out to all the governors of the thirteen states at the close of the Revolution in 1783." Then he rose and held up his glass. "A silent toast, in honor of General Washington."

All were quiet, absorbed in their own thoughts as they ate. It was Paul who broke the silence. "What always gets me about the founders is how many of them underestimated or even completely missed the threat of a tyrannical federal government. When do 'subordination and obedience' have to give way to rebellion? What say you, Evan?"

"I'm with the Federalists on this one. Rebellion is a last resort. Our revolutionary ancestors were really rolling the dice when they decided to break free from England. No subsequent rebellion in the history of the world has turned out so happily. The rebels of 1776 saw themselves as asserting their rights as Englishmen. Those rights are now under assault as never before. When the media denounce the term 'Anglo-American law' as a manifestation of racism, you know that our very civilization is under assault.

"The enemies of America are willing to use, as they say, 'any means necessary,' but we defenders of a tradition of lawful governance must be careful not to become like our adversaries."

"True," replied Paul, "but there comes a point where the barons have to confront King John, and King John is not going to come to terms except at sword point."

Evan nodded. "Let's hope it won't come to that."

"These are very dangerous times," said Wanda.

When the dinner dishes had been cleared, the whole company remained seated at the table. Wanda was breathing heavily, as if more and more anxious. "I sense a great disturbance," she said, almost in a whisper. "A disturbance *among the dead*!" She pushed back her chair and walked to a dresser, from a drawer of which she removed a number of objects and carried them to the table.

"Join with me now," said Wanda. "There are too many questions. We must consult the departed."

"Oh, come on," objected Sidney. "Are you talking about a séance? You're kidding, right? And if the 'departed' had the answer all along, why didn't you ask them sooner?"

"Something has changed now. Before, I didn't know what or whom to ask. And besides, parting the Veil is not a parlor game. There is a price to be paid." She looked older and wearier as she spoke these last words.

Wanda and the others sat silently. The group totaled seven: Wanda, Paul, Linda, Sidney, Joe, and the Fitzgeralds.

"Now," said Wanda, "I want you all to place your hands flat on the table, with each hand touching the hand of whoever is sitting next to you. In this manner, we are all connected." In front of Sidney, she placed a small, rectangular mirror with a gilt frame. The mirror tilted slightly upwards.

"You will be our medium tonight," Wanda said, looking directly at Sidney.

Sidney nodded her assent, but all of them shifted nervously in their chairs. From the table before her, Wanda took up a small antique knife with a bone handle and made a slight gash on her own palm. As the cut started to bleed, she let the blood drip onto the surfaces of two short, thick tallow candles, which she positioned on the south and north sides of the mirror. She wrapped her hand in a white handkerchief to stop the bleeding and smiled weakly at the others.

"The worst part is over, at least for me," she said.

Next, she placed a small magnet on the west side of the mirror and lit the two candles. The group waited expectantly, but Wanda remained silent. There was a leather-bound volume in front of her with a cross on the cover. She opened the book to a page marked with a purple ribbon:

I Samuel 28, then placed the Bible, opened to that verse, on the east side of the mirror.

"Please do not release your hands, and do not speak or cry out during the time we have allotted for this séance," she instructed. "Tonight, we attempt to contact the restless dead. We seek the soul of Edgar Allan Poe, who is trapped in time, conscious of loss and filled with hatred from life, and who has not yet completely separated from our world. He died an abnormal death, the victim of a foul murder, and is restless. We ask that he present himself tonight." She rang a bell, and they waited.

The only light in the room came from the two candles, the separate dying embers of the fire, and the wan rays of a full moon that filtered through the windows. A door banged in the back of the house, then banged again. There was a silken, sad, uncertain rustling in the back hall. The candles flared with a deathly blue light. A dark form loomed in the doorway and seemed to spread raven wings as it swept into the room. Sidney gasped and squeezed the hands of her companions. The thing flapped twice, then stepped into the candlelight. The phantom resolved itself into a dapper, black-clad man with a moustache.

"One does prefer to make a dramatic entrance," he said. "Especially at a *séance!*" He pronounced the word with an exaggerated French accent as if he found it ridiculous. All his attention seemed to be upon Sidney, to whom he made a graceful bow. "Do continue holding hands. I think that's required. But let us agree at the outset: if *you* don't ask me to knock once for yes and twice for no, *I* won't exert my unearthly powers to make you dance ring-around-the-rosy until you drop dead.

"You may imagine that a soul that has passed beyond this world would have no more use for the silly bickerings and idle speculations of the living, but I must confess that a bit of posthumous recognition—you know, flowers, bottles of aqua vitae, and the like—are balm even in Gilead. (Cognac is a peculiar selection, but the thought is dearer than the gift.) Contrariwise, the robbery of one's grave is apt to produce a certain amount of acrimony on the part of the man whose grave is being robbed. Has no one learned anything from all the unnecessary hauntings and mummies' curses down through the centuries, all brought about by the living taking liberties with the property of the dead? No? I take your silence as acknowledgement that the answer is as obvious as the question was rhetorical."

Wanda spoke, "Mr. Poe, will you be so kind as to indulge us by answering a few questions?"

"Madam," the shade replied, "As I am not disposed to howl or shriek, if we do not engage in conversation, the visit could prove tedious."

"Sir," asked Dr. Fitzgerald, "If I may ask, what were the materials that you instructed your cousin Neilson to bury with your remains? Did you discover the secret of physical immortality?"

The specter smiled wryly. "It is a marvel that Neilson, that self-righteous dimwit, followed the plain instructions on the package at all; but by the time he did so, it was no longer to any purpose. You see, there were two phials, each containing a powerful tincture of who knows what fungal and alkaloidal compounds, which I bought from a mysterious foreign gentleman as insurance against the horror of being buried whilst still alive. My reasoning went thus: if I awoke to my worst nightmare, premature interment, I should have the means at hand to put an end to my suffering. As soon as I had these phials, I opened one and applied a drop of the stuff to my tongue. At first, I experienced the utmost gaiety, and I capered about in the most ludicrous manner, throwing the whole room into disorder. Then I must have lost consciousness, for I awoke a day later after experiencing a spectacular and dizzying flight among the stars. I could see the whole

The Sacred Fury

Universe exploding and expanding. Kepler's laws and indeed the whole grand scheme of astronomy came clear to me, and I sat down straightaway to write *Eureka*. But first, I sealed the tops of the phials with red wax and wrapped them up with instructions that they should be buried with my remains, never suspecting that my mortal clay would be stuffed into the earth with as much ceremony as that of a dead dog, *without* the potions, mind you, which my imbecile cousin saw fit to place in the coffin only after a quarter century had passed!

"As for the idea that I discovered the secret of immortality, it is ever the fate of the literary man to learn what he *really* meant only by reading his critics. I may have told a few acquaintances, in a *jocular* way, that I had found out a means of *defeating the grave*. What they made of it is their own fault, not mine. Oh, and I could not forbear placing a note in each bottle. The note in a bottle, you will admit, is a conceit of universal popularity wherever man has discovered the written word. These little phials had room only for short Latin epigrams; so, I used a couple of my favorites. Was my intent mischievous? I leave that to the critics."

"And your cipher: 'to drink is death.' You gave it to Thompson. What did you mean by it?"

"I thought he needed a little puzzle to exercise the arithmetical part of his brain. The saying was no more than what I told myself upon promising my dear Elmira that alcohol

249

would never again pass my lips. It proved to be a prophecy, and not only for me, as you may soon learn."

Wanda opened her mouth as if to speak, but the ghost raised a hand.

"Even a restless shade grows weary of talk. I have dire vengeance yet to wreak ere my remains lie again at rest. Farewell!" He spread his arms wide, then paused.

"Oh, yes, and one last piece of advice: *Never bet the devil your head!*" His inky form swept across the table, and the candles guttered wildly and went out.

Wanda, her eyes wide, called after him, "We thank you for the honor of your presence!" Then she closed the Bible.

The full moon continued to suffuse the room with its ghostly light. Sidney and Linda stepped out into the night air. They had not let go of each other's hand. Each felt the need to hold onto the world of the living. An eerie stillness surrounded them, a tense expectancy. Even the frogs had fallen silent. Stars shone through the chill, clear air. There was a heavy dew that glistened like frost on the grass.

In Baltimore, there was a fog. No one could remember a fog so dense, not even grizzled longshoremen who had seen the Old Bay Line steamers puff up a pillar of smoke by day and the furnaces of Sparrows Point blast out a pillar of fire by night. It had begun with wisps of vapor arising from the river, pale and ragged white shapes that glided over the water. Up the Patapsco they came, past a dark and vacant fortress built by Robert E. Lee and named after a signer of the great Declaration. They glided over the spot where Francis Scott Key wrote his famous poem, and along the "shore dimly seen," where Baltimore's defenders sheltered through the night against naval bombshells and Congreve rockets two long centuries ago. Some few crept over the ramparts and into the dank cells where President Lincoln shut up his political prisoners. Rank upon rank, the mist wraiths gathered, until the ghostly throng, like a wall of cloud, pressed upon the heart of the city itself.

There were few traffic accidents. Though drivers could barely discern shapes ten feet away, it was past midnight, and almost no cars were on the road. The fog shrouded street lights, traffic lights, and the tall fence that had gone up around Westminster Hall and its graveyard. Armand Black paced irritably before the open grave of Edgar Allan Poe. He held a monogrammed handkerchief over his nose to keep out the diesel exhaust.

"Ease it down, okay, okay," shouted the foreman over the roar of the excavator.

There was a clatter and a crash as one of the chains came loose. Black instinctively put his arms up in front of his face as the coffin slipped, landed on its end, and burst apart. "Idiots!" he screamed. Lowering his hands, he thought he saw someone standing between him and the smashed coffin. A black silhouette in the fog, nothing more. The figure's clothing was of an antiquated cut. No one was supposed to be here. A no-trespassing sign had been posted.

"Ahem," said Black. The dark figure made no response. "Ahem!" he said again, somewhat louder.

The foreman shouted, "Hey! Hey, you there, the gentleman says 'ahem!'"

The figure turned, still no more than a shadow against the work lights, whose brilliance produced a haze that obscured more than it revealed. "I find," said the shadow, "that remarks of this laconic nature are nearly unanswerable. Are you in need of gargling oil, or are you endeavoring to speak in the manner of men but failing in the attempt?"

Black was near to bursting with impatience, and he did not appreciate the tone of the stranger's remark. "The last thing I need," he said, "is some joker messing up an important archaeological dig."

The shadow seemed to grow larger. It spoke again. "Oh! Rather civil that, I should say! Archaeological dig indeed! I should sooner have said a common grave robbery! Well, I've no desire to trade words with criminals."

Black took a step forward, but the intruder was gone, as if he had evaporated into the mist. A chill misgiving pierced him to the marrow, but only for a moment. This was not the first tomb he had raided. At his feet lay the stiff, dishonored shroud, and next to it was a heavy object wrapped in decaying linen. Drawing a pair of blue medical gloves from his pocket, he pulled them on and tore apart the coffin and its satin lining. There was nothing else inside. He had already rifled Mrs. Clemm's coffin and the smaller box containing the bones of Virginia. Nothing of interest was buried with the females. Slipping the linen package into a clear plastic bag, he hurried to the secure garage where he had parked his car.

No sooner had he disappeared across the street than the machine operator began shouting, "Ow, hey! Something's got hold of my hair!"

The foreman squinted through the fog. All he could see was a dim figure flailing around inside the cab of the excavator. The machine's claw began to rise, then crashed down against a gravestone. "What the hell are you doing?" screamed the foreman as the claw shot forward and threw him backward into the dark pit of Poe's grave. Without a pause, the giant mechanical arm swung in a wide arc and knocked a hole in the corner of Westminster Hall. Still wailing and swatting at a vague shadow behind him, the driver hurled himself out of the cab and fled into the fog.

Armand Black noticed that his hands were shaking and damp as he applied his right eye to the retinal scanner in the back corridor at GOOD headquarters. His fine BMW had come within an ace of skidding off the road, and he feared that its front end might have been knocked out of alignment by the low outcrop of mica-schist that had arrested his slide. Chambers was waiting for him at the top of the private stairway.

"The Chair has been awaiting your arrival," announced the secretary. His tone was such that if he had said, "You're late!" or "Obviously you took your time getting here," he could not have conveyed deeper disapproval. Chambers himself, though, had only one speed, and he shuffled slowly to the great door with its dragon carvings. There was a subtle click as a sensor detected the chip implanted in the back of the secretary's right hand; the latch released; and the smart door consented to be opened.

The office was dimly lit. A few candle flames danced on the desk and reflected in the blackness of the picture window. The Chair sat hunched forward, his mouth half open, with a gleam of spittle running down one corner. His eyes were fixed at, or perhaps somewhere beyond, the Samurai. He spoke in a whisper that was almost a hiss. "Bring it to me!"

Black stepped forward. He was about to say something, but the expression, or lack of expression, in his employer's eyes filled him with such foreboding that he merely placed his package on the desk and stepped back.

"Open it, you fool!" rasped the Chair.

Obeying with such haste that he rapped his knee against a protruding metal knob on the desk, Black opened the gallon-sized zip-lock plastic bag and extracted something wrapped in linen. Inside the fragile linen wrapping was a packet of lead foil. He paused.

"Go on!" commanded the Chair.

The lead foil unfolded to reveal two identical phials with red wax seals. Each contained some kind of brown liquid.

"I think we should have these analyzed," said Dr. Black.

The Chair drew in a rattling breath. "There's no time." His mouth assumed an expression remarkably similar to the Samurai's. "Chambers, I need you." His pale hands took up first one phial, then the other, scraping off the wax and extracting the corks with his yellow, curving fingernails.

Chambers stood before the desk, his eyes wide.

"That's right, drink it," wheezed the Chair.

And Chambers did just that. Black was not sure whether to admire him for courage or despise him for folly; but drink it he did. He handed the empty bottle to the historian and began moving his arms around. He lifted first one leg, then the other, then stretched his back. A light of pure joy appeared in his eyes. "I can't believe it!" he exclaimed. "I can't believe

it!" He began capering as if he were dancing a jig. "I feel...
I feel *young* again!"

The Chair detached his eyes from the Samurai for the first
time since the others had entered the room. He closed his
mouth and wiped it with the back of his hand. He watched
his secretary with a skeptical expression.

"Look, sir!" cried the old secretary, who was now doing
jumping-jacks. "Here, Dr. Black, feel my pulse."

Black held his fingers on the sweaty left wrist as one
might grasp someone else's discarded banana peel. "Normal," he said, wiping his fingers on the man's coat sleeve as
if he were readjusting the fabric. Out of the corner of his eye,
he saw Pyknos drain the other bottle in a single gulp. He still
had the first empty bottle in his left hand, and he held it up to
the light of a candle. Inside was a slip of paper.

"I believe there's a note in here!" he said, reaching for a
box of paperclips. He straightened one out and managed to
extract the paper. He blotted it on the discarded linen wrapping. It appeared to be parchment, with delicate writing in
India ink. Chambers was digging at the other bottle and produced an identical scrap of paper.

The secretary seemed almost giddy. "Letters in bottles!
What fun! It's like fortune cookies! Here, what do they say?"

Pyknos rose from his chair with a sharp cry, but it was a cry of
pleasure. He too began to dance around the room, albeit unsteadily.

Black held the parchments under a candle and read. His face grew a shade paler as he did so. The first message was "*Nemo me impune lacessit.*" The second was "*Quem Dei volunt perdere, prius dementant.*"[3] The candle guttered, and its flame took on a bluish cast.

"Ahem," said Dr. Black. "Gentlemen, I'm afraid this may not be good news."

The dancers were now holding hands, swinging each other round and round, and giggling, "Hoo, hoo, Chambers! Well done!" and "Excellent pirouette, Sir! Ha, ha!"

A shadow passed between them, and the character of their exclamations began to change, "Ho, ho, ooh! Ouch! You pulled my nose!" "You boxed my ear!" "Oh, gouge my eye, will you!"

In an instant, the giddy laughter became feral snarling, and they were beginning to claw at each other with their nails. Black started toward the door. He struck his right shoulder against something. The Samurai. It was rocking back and forth on its pedestal. The two combatants turned, distracted by the movement.

"You!" shouted Pyknos, and it sounded as if all the demons of hell were disgorging their fury. "You did this to me!" And he snatched the dagger off the desk and came straight for Armand.

---

[3] "No one wounds me with impunity" (cf. The Cask of Amontillado) and "Whom the gods would destroy, they first make mad."

Now, Dr. Black had done some fencing in his time, and he was still a keen tennis player; so he knew how to move out of the way. But the ferocity of the attack terrified him, and his antagonist was preparing for a second charge. This time, the poignard left a rent in the side of his coat. He snatched a sword off the wall. It was one of those two-handed affairs with a long hilt, but Armand held it like a tennis racket.

As Pyknos lowered his head and charged for a third time, Black executed a powerful backhand stroke, which would have put a nice leftward curve on a tennis ball. Under the circumstances, however, it lopped the Chair's head clean off, and the head rolled (with a rightward spin, having been struck on the following, rather than the leading, edge) under the Hinoki-wood desk.

There was blood all over the floor. Chambers was clawing at the Samurai armor and shouting something about the devil. Black backed against the door and was relieved to hear the latch release. Proximity detector inside, chip reader outside, thank God! He tossed the sword in the general direction of Chambers and fled down the stairs.

At the foot of the stairs, he ran headlong into Livvy Bollard. He recoiled at the contact.

The captain was in a foul mood. She had learned that Joe, who was supposed to lead her to the enemies of Pyknos, had decided to spend his time riding an MTA bus. The Chair would not be pleased.

"What's the matter with you?" she shouted. "Don't you... " Then she actually looked at him. The blood spattered on his dark suit was not evident in the dim corridor, but the expression on his face was enough to stop her cold.

"They're killing each other!" gasped Black. "In the Chair's office. He and Chambers!"

This was precisely the sort of emergency for which Captain Bollard, Chief Security Officer, was fully prepared. She drew her nine-millimeter Glock and bounded up the stairs. The chip reader responded to her touch, and her booted foot flung the heavy door open. Her mind took in the situation in an instant. The headless body of Klaus Pyknos lay on the floor. The head was nowhere to be seen. To her immediate right, Chambers was shredding the Samurai armor with a bloody sword and shouting about the devil. The great blade was poised high above his head, ready for the next stroke.

"Drop it! Drop the weapon!" she shouted. The frenzied eyes of the private secretary gleamed red around the edges as he turned toward the sound of her voice. With a cry of pure hatred, he took a step toward her. Four shots roared in rapid succession as he brought the blade down on the top of her head, and both combatants fell to the ground, their blood flowing out to merge with that of their employer in one dark red pool.

Armand Black took a few steps down the hall. He felt suddenly faint. Stumbling, he steadied himself by catching hold of a door handle. It gave, and the door flew open. Sitting slumped over a desk was his young friend Dylan. There were dark rings under his eyes. A smashed computer lay on the floor, and the potted ficus tree in the corner smelled like a sewer. The odor snapped the historian out of his swoon. He had seen enough of GOOD's methods to surmise that Dylan had refused to cooperate.

"Come on," he urged. "Let's get you out of here," He helped Dylan to his feet, and together they hurried down the gray corridor and through the central hall of the mansion. From behind them came a howling, as of a great wind. They quickened their steps.

The little company at the farm house near Rising Sun huddled around the wood stove in the living room. Wanda sat with her eyes closed, in her customary meditative pose, with palms turned upward to receive a communication. Paul sat beside her, with a glass of port. All were silent, occupied with their own thoughts. The Pekingese dogs had found willing laps to lie on and were snoring softly. Suddenly, Wanda gave a little gasp.

"It is over," she said, as if in a dream. "The crisis has passed. Klaus Pyknos, or what remained of him, is dead. The

designs of the Evil One have been thwarted, at least for now."
Opening her eyes, she smiled. "I trust the spirit of Poe has
taken his revenge. When the accounts of today's events appear in the papers and on the news networks, the externalities
will appear, which will no doubt be interesting enough. But
the *meaning* of the events will be known to us alone."

"Apart from knowing and watching and waiting," complained Paul, "I can't see that we've accomplished much. We
weren't at all instrumental in bringing about the Chair's down-
fall, and by trying to interfere, we let poor Joe fall into their
hands, with nothing to show for it. And won't the whole vile
enterprise of GOOD keep right on going without Pyknos?"

"I believe that Evan's alteration of Poe's coded message
tipped the balance. And he could never have known of its significance without Sidney's visions, which would not have
come to us if Rose had not sent her here," said Wanda.

"And," added Sidney, "Thanks to Rose, Paul showed up
just in time to save *me* from that Captain Bollard."

Wanda nodded and smiled feebly. Her eyes were focused
far away. "My children," she said, "we wind our way through
a dark valley, where temples fall into decay and slimy things
creep among the ruins, defiling the icons and the holy altars.
It may seem to you that in merely keeping to the true path,
you are doing little. But when you uphold the faith, speak the
truth, and love and support this extended family, you carry

forward the sacred flame. The struggle will be long. The minions of the Enemy grow ever more violent in their assaults on those who stand against their ruler, who is the Lord of Lies. But have no fear, for yours is the Lord of Truth.

"Be strong in the Truth. But know that my time among you is not long."

"No!" interrupted Paul. "Don't say that!"

Wanda raised her hand. "Peace, my dear. I am not yet ready to cross over." She patted his hand. "Still, the day must come when your hand shall slip from mine, and you must go on. But you will not be alone."

The fire crackled in the stove, and all the dogs gazed up at Wanda with sad brown eyes.

———

At the headquarters of GOOD, the howling rose to a tormented wail that seemed to sink downward into the earth itself. Then there was only an eerie silence. And in that silence, at a secret level deep below the security offices, a long array of red, light-emitting diodes blinked three times, paused in utter darkness, and then, one by one, blazed steadily. The self-organizing, artificial Mind of Klaus Pyknos had reawakened from its artificial sleep.

End Note

1   "Intersectionality" was coined by a black feminist. There is a hierarchy to the coalition
    of the oppressed. Think of all categories of supposedly oppressed people (non-white,
    non-male, disabled, etc.) as overlapping sets. Whoever suffers the most different kinds
    of oppression wins.

2   Derrida and Foucault: Jacques Derrida (July 15, 1930-October 9, 2004) was a Spa-
    nish Jew born in Algeria, and Paul-Michel Foucault (October 15, 1926-June 25, 1984)
    was a French bourgeois with a penchant for homoerotic sadomasochism (he died of
    AIDS). Both were radicals who developed and promoted the academically influential
    notions of post-structuralism and postmodernism. Rejecting all ideas of traditional mo-
    rality and reducing all human relations to exploiter vs. exploited, they are part of the
    philosophical pantheon of Cultural Marxism, which seeks to upend every aspect of
    normal human life by inciting an unending conflict between the oppressed (everyone
    who isn't a heterosexual white male) and the oppressors (everyone who is a heterosex-
    ual white male).

3   "Beggars full of lice." Michel Houellebecq (born February 26, 1956) is a French au-
    thor whose novels grapple with the problem of mass immigration and the clash of
    Muslim and European cultures. The quote is from Platforme (2001). Soumission
    (2015) carries the theme into the future.

4   Cousin Neilson Poe commissioned a very ordinary grave marker from Baltimore stone
    carver Hugh Sisson in 1860. Just when the marker was completed and ready to be
    moved to the cemetery, a train inexplicably derailed from the Northern Central line
    and ran through Sisson's yard. The only thing irreparably damaged was Poe's head-
    stone. Apparently, the poet's restless ghost found the marker inadequate.

5   John Reuben Thompson (October 23, 1823-April 30, 1873) was born in Richmond and
    presumably met Evan Fitzgerald, Sr. at the University of Virginia. In 1847, Thompson
    became editor of the Southern Literary Messenger, which his father purchased for him.
    He was one of the last people in Richmond to see Edgar Allan Poe alive. Poe handed
    him the manuscript of Annabel Lee as described in the letter. The presence of an en-

closed cryptogram may come as news to Poe scholars. A sickly man, Thompson was too ill to remain in wartime Richmond and escaped through the Union blockade to live in London, where he edited a pro-Confederate paper. He returned to the U.S. in 1867 to work for William Cullen Bryant at the Evening Post in New York, where he died of tuberculosis. Thompson gave lectures on Poe in the late 1860's and was the first to claim that members of a 'lawless political club' had imprisoned Poe in a cellar overnight, drugged him or stupefied him with cheap liquor, dragged him around to cast votes in eleven different wards, and then left him helplessly intoxicated and close to death.

[6] Lieutenant Colonel William H. Watson (1808-1846), a Maryland hero of the Mexican War, died at the Battle of Monterey.